THE SUTHERLIN FILES

DARK CURRENT

ASHLEY FARLEY

Also By Ashley Farley

The Sutherlin Files

Dark Current Rising

Dark Current

Dark Current Reckoning

Soul Seekers

Return to Marsh Hollow

Where Light lingers

When Sparks Fly

Cupid's Countdown

Messy Under the Mistletoe

The First Last Kiss

Sandy Island

Southern Discomfort

Beneath the Carolina Sun

Southern Simmer

Marsh Point

Long Journey Home

Echoes of the Past

Songbird's Second Chance

Heart of Lowcountry

After the Storm

Weekend on Sullivan's Island

Virginia Vineyards

Love Child

Blind Love

Forbidden Love

Love and War

Palmetto Island

Muddy Bottom

Change of Tides

Lowcountry on My Mind

Sail Away

Hope Springs Series

Dream Big, Stella!

Show Me the Way

Mistletoe and Wedding Bells

Matters of the Heart

Road to New Beginnings

Stand Alone

Scent of Magnolia

On My Terms

Tangled in Ivy

Lies that Bind

Life on Loan

Only One Life

Home for Wounded Hearts

Nell and Lady

Sweet Tea Tuesdays

Sweeney Sisters Series

Chapter One

I'm seated in the front row of the courtroom, where I've been all week. Scout is curled at my feet. We've been inseparable since Addie disappeared two months ago. Only eight weeks? Hard to believe. It feels like a lifetime ago when I walked away from my so-called life in Richmond—a failed marriage, a nonexistent social life, and a suspension for behavior unbecoming a detective.

Beside me, my father sits rapt, as if the courtroom still belongs to him. His mind is slipping, but today he's as alert as I've seen him since I came home in early September. Before his retirement two years ago, the Honorable Hollis Sutherlin ruled from this very bench for more than two decades. Tidewell loved him. He's still widely respected by its citizens. He ran a tight ship—iron fist, fair heart—and somehow turned half his convicted felons into Sunday school teachers.

The current judge, Vernon Tate, wears black robes and pretends to care about the law. I glance over at him now, nodding off with his hands resting on his ample belly. Lawson Briggs—the commonwealth's attorney—did everything in his power to get a change of venue, arguing that half the town had already made up its mind. Tate denied it—claiming he trusted our fine citizens to be fair—then rushed the case to trial so fast our heads are still spinning.

Briggs looks the part today—every inch the hotshot attorney in an immaculate gray suit, starched white shirt, and blue striped tie. Clean-shaven, sandy hair brushed back from his face, he holds the jury spellbound as he walks them through Addie's final hours.

The fight with her husband, Clay—the accused. The fight Clay claims never happened—when he begged her to lie about the paternity of her unborn child. Her decision to walk the dog along the waterfront instead of through town, as was her habit. A visit to her lover's houseboat. Another argument. Ben testified that he pleaded with her to leave Clay and marry him so they could raise their baby together. Then her disappearance. A glimpse of Clay's truck on the marina's security camera. Addie's dog found the next morning near the marsh. Three days later, her body discovered in the old boathouse at Founders State Park.

Dad leans in and whispers, "This jury will acquit."

I snap my head toward him. "How can you be sure?"

He cuts his eyes at me as if to say, *Are you really asking me that?*

Dread settles heavy in my chest. I've been worried about this since the start of the trial. Tate kept a tight grip on jury selection—dismissing Briggs's strikes, overruling every challenge to the women who blushed when Clay smiled at them during questioning. The nine chosen women are nurses, choir directors, and schoolteachers ranging in age from twenty-nine to sixty-three.

Of the three men, one is a retired mail carrier who will go with the majority. Another is an insurance agent who plays golf with Tate. Our only hope—Travis Keene, thirty-eight, an HVAC contractor—was called out of town late last night for a family emergency. I don't believe in coincidences. Not anymore.

Alternate number one has taken his place—Earl Minton, forty-eight, vice president at Tidewell Community Bank, the kind of man who calls Tate *sir* even off the clock.

Scout's legs twitch, and she whines softly in her sleep. Those seated around us glance down at her, smiling—she's become something of a local celebrity. Dogs aren't allowed in the courtroom. The bailiff has tried more than once to make her leave, but she's my therapy dog now. Where I go, she goes.

Yesterday, during Clay's testimony, Scout sat rigid in the chair beside me, a low growl rumbling in her throat. She was there on the night of the murder. She doesn't need proof.

My eyes meet Dad's over her head, and we share a quiet moment. He folds his hand over mine.

Briggs wraps up his closing arguments—articulate, measured, every point lined up like soldiers. I can't find a single flaw, and neither can Dad, judging by his deep exhale and the way he finally settles back in his chair.

After a brief recess, Tate turns the floor over to Brock Thornton —the high-priced, big-city criminal defense attorney Clay's daddy hired. His tailored navy suit probably costs more than my car, his hair shellacked into place like he's auditioning for a *GQ* spread. Even his watch gleams like it came with its own security detail. But I'll give him this—he's good. A master at rearranging the truth until it sounds like gospel. Worth every one of his thousand-dollar-an-hour minutes.

Tate gives the jury their final instructions before sending them off to deliberate.

I watch Briggs make a beeline for the back door. I don't follow. I know that look—he needs room to breathe. Since Clay's arrest, I've been helping build the case. Late nights, cold takeout, shared silences. I've earned my place beside him—even if neither of us knows what to call it yet.

I turn to Dad. "Now we wait. Want me to take you home?"

He shakes his head. "The jury won't be out long. Let's grab some lunch—our place, my treat."

I smile. "Our place, it is."

A mob scene waits outside the courthouse. The sidewalk divides the two camps—*Justice for Addie* and *Free Clay*.

I take Dad by the arm, guiding him toward the parking lot as voices call out. *Guilty or innocent, Judge?*

By the time we reach my Bronco, his hands are trembling. "Why don't I take you home, Dad? I'll call ahead and have Lally fix us some chili or tomato soup."

"No, Lane." He gives me a look that warns me not to argue. "We can order soup at Cooter's. I want to be close when the verdict comes in."

"Okay, if you're sure." When I reach to fasten his seatbelt, he brushes me aside.

"I've got it. I can buckle it myself."

I lift my hands in surrender. "Just trying to help," I say, letting Scout into the back seat.

Dad's been sharp all morning—leaning forward, hanging on every word. Now that spark is gone, replaced by a vacant stare that chills me more than the wind off the bay. I tell myself it's just exhaustion, but the denial tastes stale even as I think it.

We ride the short distance to the city marina in silence. I help Dad out of the Bronco, and we walk to the center of the main dock.

Our place is everyone's place in town—the iconic spot for birthdays, football Saturdays, and every ordinary day worth making special. Slip 99 sits at the end of the dock, its wide windows offering a sweeping view of Oyster Bay. Fans turn lazily above the tongue-and-groove pine ceiling, stirring the scent of fried oysters and beer. Sunlight bounces off the water, flooding the dining room with a soft amber glow. The wooden floors are worn smooth by salt and stories—first dates, breakups, homecomings, and the occasional bar fight. If these boards could talk, they'd probably roll their eyes and order another round.

Cooter and Frankie hustle behind the long bar, pulling drafts and serving up platters of raw oysters. Cooter—owner and head bartender—spots me and lifts both hands, fingers crossed. Word has spread—the jury's out.

Briggs and I have spent most of our lunches at this bar, slurping oysters and talking strategy. Cooter and Frankie were right there with us—sounding boards, moral support—never letting our glasses run dry.

The place is buzzing, half the town high on Halloween and the rest on courtroom adrenaline. The words that greet us aren't *trick or treat*, but *guilty or innocent*.

Darlene, thick gray braid over one shoulder, takes our orders —she-crab soup and sweet tea for us, a hamburger patty for Scout. Friends stop by to speak to Dad. He's pleasant but guarded, his smile slow to arrive.

I realize that he might not remember them.

Across the room, Briggs stands just inside the door, scanning the crowd. When he spots us, he heads over and extends a hand to Dad.

"Good to see you in the courtroom today, Judge," Briggs says with a chuckle. "Although I admit, your presence made me a little nervous."

"You certainly didn't show it. You did an outstanding job. You have a bright future ahead of you, young man."

Young man? Does he not remember Lawson Briggs—his oldest son's best childhood friend?

I gesture to the empty seat beside me. "Wanna join us?"

Briggs hesitates. I can tell he wants to talk, just not in front of Dad. He stuffs his hands into his pockets. "Thanks, but I'm a nervous wreck. I'm no fun to be around right now. I'll grab something from the bar. I might even get it to go."

I smile softly. "I'll catch up with you after lunch."

"Sounds good." He squeezes my shoulder before heading to the bar.

I wait until he's out of earshot. "That was Lawson Briggs, Dad. The commonwealth's attorney. He was Tommy's best friend."

Recognition flickers. "Lawson, of course. His name slipped my mind." His eyes scan the room. "Is Tommy with him?"

My blood runs cold. The noise of the restaurant dulls to a hum, like I'm underwater. Dad is searching the room for a ghost, and I can't bring myself to correct him. Maybe letting him believe Tommy is still out there is kinder than the truth.

Movement by the door catches my eye—a flash of sandy hair, a glimpse of gray suit. Briggs is gone. His stool empty. His drink untouched.

From behind the bar, Cooter's voice cuts through the chatter. "Jury's back!"

Chapter Two

D ad is silent as we head back toward the square. His eyelids flutter, then his chin drops to his chest. I should probably take him home, but I gave the caregiver the day off, and I can't leave him alone. Besides, by the time I drive out to the farm and back, I'll miss the verdict.

I nudge him awake. "This is bad, right? Taking less than an hour to reach a verdict?"

"Not necessarily," he says, rubbing his eyes and placing his head against the headrest. "It means the jurors all agreed—one way or the other."

I tighten my grip on the steering wheel. "Probably Clay's way."

"Probably," he mutters, eyes closing again.

Anger surges through me as I continue to the courthouse. Clay killed Addie. I'm as certain of that as I am my own name. Her wedding rings were missing when her body was discovered. I found her wedding band in the marsh—near where we believe she disappeared, where I found Scout the next day. And when I arrested Clay weeks later, he stood in that same spot and dangled the engagement ring—his grandmother's diamond—smiling as he tossed it into the water.

The image of that ring hitting the water still burns in my mind as I search for somewhere to park. The courthouse lot is packed—news vans lining the curb, half of Tidewell hunting for spaces.

I circle twice before giving up and sliding the Bronco into a space marked RESERVED FOR SHERIFF'S OFFICE. Technically, I'm not on duty. But old habits die hard, and my badge still opens doors. Normally, Dad would protest, arguing that I shouldn't take advantage of the perks when I'm not on the clock. But today, he just stares out the window, lost somewhere I can't follow.

I make a split-second decision to leave Scout in the car, windows cracked. It's in the sixties today—she'll be fine for a little while. I'm grateful for that choice the moment we see the crowd inside. The courtroom is packed, air thick with perfume, coffee, and nerves.

My usual seat behind Briggs is taken. Dad and I squeeze into the standing-room-only section at the back. When the locals spot him, they shuffle and shift, creating a space for the judge. Tidewell still knows how to honor its own.

The rear door opens, and the bailiff ushers in the jurors. The women smile shyly at Clay, and the men wear the smug looks of a job well done. It's over. They've acquitted him.

Briggs knows it too. His shoulders sag, his jaw tight, eyes fixed on the table in front of him.

"Has the jury reached a verdict?" Tate asks.

The foreperson—Renee Mullins, middle-aged nurse wearing a red cardigan and pearls—rises. "We have, Your Honor."

She passes the folded paper to the bailiff, who delivers it to Tate. The judge scans it, expression unreadable, then hands it off to the clerk. The room holds its breath.

The clerk clears his throat. "We, the jury, find the defendant, Clayton Dalton, *not guilty* of murder in the first degree."

Gasps ripple through the gallery. Clay exhales sharply, head bowed in mock humility as his attorney pats him on the back.

Beside me, Dad's alert again, but his voice carries the fatigue of a man who's seen too much. "Justice missed her mark today.

That young man wears his guilt the way he wears that suit—like it belongs to him."

"Don't you worry, Dad. I'm not done with Clay Dalton yet," I say, but my words are swallowed by the chaos erupting around us.

The courthouse doors slam open, and the press surges forward, tripping over each other in their scramble to be first with the news. Friends and family swarm Clay, hugging him and slapping him on the back like he's the hometown football hero again.

The town is eager to forget the tragedy that has consumed it these past few weeks.

My heart breaks for Briggs as I watch him gather his files. Is he swiping at his eyes? I wouldn't blame him for crying. He poured everything he had into this case. We both did.

While this isn't the outcome we hoped for, we should face it together. But there's a sea of people between us, and I need to get Dad out of here before he gets trampled.

In front of the courthouse, Addie's supporters shout *Justice for Addie,* but their cries are swallowed by the whoops and hollering of the *Free Clay* crowd.

As we make our way toward the parking lot, people stop to shake Dad's hand. He greets the faces he's known all his life with polite nods and a vacant expression that tightens my chest.

He's quiet during the fifteen-minute drive, waiting until we're turning onto the farm road to speak his mind. "You did everything you could, Laney Bug. The evidence was solid. But this case was compromised from the start. Tate should've insisted on a change of venue."

He turns away, looking out the window. "I've seen this coming for years. The Old Guard will stop at nothing to control this town. Tidewell's more divided than folks realize. It's a sinking ship, and the Old Guard is still at the helm."

An icy finger slides down my back. On the rare occasion Dad mentions the Old Guard, he does so in a whisper, as if saying the words out loud might bring harm to his family.

I pass through the tunnel of river birch trees, their pale bark flashing in the afternoon sunlight. Our old farmhouse waits at the end, weathered by generations of Sutherlins—remodeled, repainted, patched over the years, yet still clinging to the same stubborn character that runs in our blood.

Inside, the house is dark and still, holding its breath the way old places do when they remember too much. Scout trails me through the mudroom into the kitchen, her tail drooping as if she senses the disastrous outcome of the thing we've been working so hard for these past weeks. I expect to find Lally at the stove or folding laundry. Then I remember. She texted earlier to say she'd left for the courthouse and wouldn't be back today.

I pull a container of her oyster stew from the fridge. The verdict interrupted our lunch, and I need to get Dad some nourishment. "I'll heat some stew, Dad. Won't take but a second."

Dad waves me off as he passes through to the family room. "Thanks, Bug, but I'm not hungry. I'll be in my study."

He disappears down the hall, leaving me standing there with the container in my hand. I stare at it a moment before returning it to the fridge. I'm not really hungry either. My stomach's too knotted to even think about food. I fill the kettle for tea instead.

I'm dunking my tea bag in a mug a few minutes later when my brother barges in, dropping his armload of groceries on the counter and surprising me with a hug.

"I'm so sorry, Laney. I was in the grocery store when I heard the verdict. I drove as fast as I could." He lets go and glances around the kitchen. "Where's Dad? Is he okay?"

"He's in his study. Aside from a few lapses of memory, he was pretty alert all morning. It took a lot out of him, though. He seems wiped out now."

Judd's brow creases. "The front door's locked, right? The bell rack in place?"

"I assume so. We came in the back." I toss the soggy tea bag in the trash. "He's probably in a deep sleep by now."

"I'll check to make sure," Judd says, disappearing into the family room.

We rigged our makeshift motion detector weeks ago—old sleigh bells strung across a rolling wardrobe rack parked by the front door. It's meant to alert us if Dad tries to wander. He hasn't in a while, but after the day we've had, I wouldn't be surprised if he got restless.

Judd's back in a flash. "You're right. Sound asleep." He unloads groceries, lining up his purchases on the counter.

"What's all this?" I ask, sweeping a hand over the bricks of cream cheese and cartons of heavy cream.

"I'm making a cheesecake."

I laugh. "You're serious about these cooking classes."

He shrugs. "Maybe I inherited Dad's culinary talents."

Hollis Sutherlin was once the most famous nonprofessional chef in the Commonwealth of Virginia. He frequently hosted politicians and other influential figures at our dining room table.

"Glad to know you've got Sutherlin blood in your veins after all," I say, mischief tugging at my lips. I tease Judd for taking after our mother—her looks, I mean. Roxie may be a knockout, but her morals are . . . well, questionable.

"You're a riot," he says, grabbing a mixing bowl from the cabinet and cracking three eggs into it.

I lean against the counter, watching him work. "What flavor cheesecake?"

"Salted caramel." He unwraps the cream cheese. "If it doesn't flop, I'll freeze it for Thanksgiving. You'll be here, right?"

"For Thanksgiving? Why wouldn't I?" I ask, sipping my tea.

"I figured now that the trial's over, you'd be heading back to Richmond."

I shake my head. "I'm not leaving you here alone to deal with Dad."

"But you have a life in Richmond. What about your job?"

"I resigned from Richmond PD a month ago," I say, barely above a whisper.

His head jerks up. "What? Why didn't you tell me?"

"I'm not sure, honestly. Even after I resigned, I wasn't sure I was going to stay."

He measures out a cup of sugar. "What changed your mind?"

"Unfinished business. Things I need to take care of." Briggs is part of that unfinished business, but I don't admit that to my brother.

His smile fades as he sets up the stand mixer. "Unfinished business that might get you killed. I was hoping you'd go back to Richmond, where you'd be safe." He glances toward the hallway, lowering his voice. "You've seen how divided this town is. Bad things are happening, Laney. No one is safe here anymore."

"All the more reason for me to stay." I straighten, lowering my mug. "What sort of bad things are you talking about?"

"A group calling themselves the Night Riders, claiming to be community protection." He snorts. "Community protection, my foot. It's about control."

I push off the counter. "It's always about control, Judd. Who are these Night Riders?"

His mouth twists. "Punks—young guys in their early twenties. They're all related, either by blood or marriage, to the Old Guard."

"Of course. It always circles back to the Old Guard. What sort of protection are they offering our community?"

"They're driving around all night, watching who comes and goes. Keeping tabs." His jaw tightens. "They harassed Hank Jenkins's daughter for walking home from work alone after midnight. And they dragged Barry Waters's son and his girlfriend out of the car when they caught them parking down by Patriots Landing." He meets my eyes. "You're a detective, Lane. You work for the sheriff's department. How is this the first you're hearing about it?"

"*Work* is the operative word. Boone hired me to get me off his back—and to keep a close eye on me while I was investigating Addie's death. I never even got a paycheck. I'm not sure where I stand with the sheriff now. I still have the badge, but I haven't stepped inside the department in weeks."

Judd lets out a slow breath, rubbing the back of his neck. "Just promise me you'll keep your head down. This isn't your fight anymore, Laney."

My jaw drops. "Clay was acquitted today, Judd. The jury found him not guilty, when I know in my heart he killed Addie. I can't let that go. This fight isn't over. If what you say is true about the Night Riders, it's escalating."

Judd doesn't respond. He just watches the stand mixer beat the eggs, round and around.

He's right about one thing—Tidewell's coming apart at the seams. And if the Old Guard's running the show, someone needs to start pulling threads.

When a moment passes and he doesn't look up, I ask, "What aren't you telling me?"

He glances around, making sure we're still alone. "I don't want Dad to know yet. But Brandy's pregnant."

I haven't felt excited about anything in so long. I barely recognize the flutters dancing across my chest. "That's great, Judd. Congratulations."

He smiles, but it fades quickly. "I wish I felt more like celebrating. It took so long for Brandy to get pregnant . . . What if something happens? Either to her or the baby?"

I slump against the counter. "Are you that worried about your safety?"

"You'll understand when you meet the Night Riders. And Clay's acquittal will make the situation escalate." He rummages through the cabinets for a springform pan. "Our lease is up at the end of November. We're thinking about moving into the guest cottage full-time. It's bigger than our apartment, and we'd both feel safer out here. Is that okay with you?"

"Of course! You don't even have to ask. I love having you on the property. You can move into the main house if you want. There are three more bedrooms upstairs just gathering dust."

He considers this for a minute, then shakes his head. "We'll be fine in the cottage for now."

I drop an arm around his shoulders. "Be happy about the baby. You deserve this."

He ducks out from under my arm. "I am happy. Truly. But I'll feel better when she's a little further along."

A thought strikes me. "Wait—did Brandy have a fertility procedure?"

"No, thank goodness. We only saw the fertility specialist once. Dr. Ellison told us nothing was wrong and to be patient. She was right."

A broad smile spreads across my face. "I can't believe I'm gonna be an aunt. I'll throw you a couple's baby shower. We'll invite everyone in town."

Judd groans. But as the mixer hums and he talks about who they'll invite, my mind drifts to Dr. Ellison. I've been too focused on helping Briggs build his case to investigate the spreadsheets I found in Addie's closet—spreadsheets that link Dr. Ellison to something sinister.

Clay can't be tried for Addie's murder again. Double jeopardy closed that door. But the spreadsheets—the columns of names, the tallies of harvested eggs—point to something else entirely. Egg trafficking. *Human* trafficking.

Clay may look clean on the surface, but there's dirt beneath the shine. And I intend to dig.

Chapter Three

I give Briggs until early evening. But when I don't hear from him, I try calling. He doesn't pick up, and I don't leave a voicemail. I wait another thirty minutes and try again. No answer. I shoot him a text.

> You okay? I'm here if you need to talk.

I stare at my screen. No dancing dots appear.

Grabbing my coat, I jog down the stairs, pausing in the doorway of Dad's study to make sure he's still asleep. Continuing to the kitchen, I find Judd admiring his cheesecake.

"Nice job," I say, eyeing it. "I need to run to town. Can you stay with Dad until I get back?"

He looks up, his brow furrowed. "What's wrong?"

"I'm worried about Briggs. He's not answering his phone."

A smirk tugs at his mouth. "What's going on with you two? You've been spending an awful lot of time together lately."

"Duh. We've been working together on Addie's case."

I slip out before he can press further. His inquisition doesn't surprise me. Briggs and I have been inseparable these past few weeks. It's a small town. People talk.

We've worked everywhere—his office, Slip 99, the Salty Bean Cafe, half the eateries on the town square. Everywhere but his house. I know he lives on Heron Bluff, the row of historic homes built into the river's hillside across from town. I just don't know the exact address.

I cross the bridge and ease down the narrow lane. I spot his silver Tahoe in front of a navy frame house with khaki shutters, white trim, and a cheerful red front door.

The man who answers the door is not the same one who commanded the courtroom only hours ago. Gone is the polished prosecutor. In his place stands a man in bare feet and rumpled clothes—a sloppy hoodie and worn jeans. His sandy waves hang loosely in his face, his eyes bloodshot and unfocused. One hand grips the doorframe—as though using it to stay upright—while the other dangles a glass of amber liquid. Bourbon is Briggs's drink of choice.

"What're you doing here, Lane? I'm busy."

I lift my phone. "Too busy to answer my calls?" Without waiting for an answer, I brush past him into the house. Nice place —leather sectional, expensive rug. But neither can compete with the view of Oyster Bay through the wall of windows. To the right, in the adjacent kitchen, dirty dishes are piled in the sink, and papers blanket the breakfast counter.

Briggs shuts the door and comes to stand beside me. "It's over, Lane. We lost."

Over? Our partnership? Our friendship?

"I heard, Briggs. I was in the courtroom." I turn to face him. "You're not alone in this. Everyone lost today. You. Me. This town. Mostly Addie. The jury decided Clay's innocent, and now he's back on the street—an officer of the law, no less. Which makes him extremely dangerous."

He sweeps an arm at the files and legal pads strewn across the counter. "What do you want me to do? I've been over the evidence a thousand times, trying to see where we went wrong."

Dad's words echo in my head. *The evidence was rock solid, but the case was compromised from the start. Tate should've insisted on a change of venue.*

"You did a brilliant job presenting the case," I say evenly. "The jury either chose not to believe it . . . or they were *instructed* not to believe it."

Briggs's head jerks up. "What does that mean?"

"You did the best you could with jury selection. But your hands were tied from the beginning. You only get so many strikes, and in a town this small, everybody's tied to somebody."

He gestures for me to get to the point.

"I think Tate swayed the jury. I sat in that courtroom all week long, watching the jurors. Memorizing their faces. Loraine Harper—dark circles from sleepless nights with a colicky baby. Patty Jo Sykes—new money, bad skin, desperate to be seen as respectable."

Briggs snorts. "That's great, Lane. I spent six weeks building a case, and you cracked it with a dermatology consult."

"You're missing my point. I didn't just study the evidence. I studied this jury. Tommy Griggs, the insurance agent, is a good ol' boy who plays golf with Tate. Joyce Rawlings and Clay were high school classmates. My sources say she was hopelessly in love with him. They even dated once." I pause, letting that land. "And Gina Crenshaw owns a hair salon. Addie was her competition. Those two despised each other. She shot death glares at Ben during his testimony. In her mind, Addie wasn't a victim—she was a woman who had an affair. She was immoral. She deserved what happened to her."

"Come on, Lane. Enough with the drama," Briggs says, draining his glass and setting it on the counter.

"You didn't see the look in her eyes." I step closer, lowering my voice. "Travis Keene was the one juror I felt certain of. I'm not buying his family emergency. And Earl Minton—alternate number one—owes Tate. Big time."

Briggs stiffens. "How so?"

"Minton's son was arrested for a DUI back in April. Kid blew a

.12. He should've lost his license, maybe his college scholarship. Tate erased the case. Not dismissed. Not reduced." I snap my fingers. "Just—gone."

"Where'd you hear this? I'm the commonwealth's attorney. I would've heard about a DUI?"

"Not necessarily. Tate and Boone only tell you what they want you to know."

Briggs's mouth tightens. "That's not how it works, Lane."

"Not in most places. But this is Tidewell." I don't give him a chance to argue. "When we agreed to go after Clay, we knew we'd be taking on the corruption rotting Tidewell from the inside out. His acquittal is just the beginning."

"Can't be done," Briggs says flatly.

My eyes widen. "So, you're just quitting?"

"Nope. I'm moving on. I've applied for an assistant position in Richmond. Bigger office. More support. Less corruption."

I stare at him, blindsided. He never mentioned leaving Tidewell. When unexpected tears fill my eyes, I move to the window and look out at the darkening sky. His view faces east. I imagine his sunrises are spectacular, mirroring the sunsets out at River Birch.

"How can you give all this up?" I ask in a small voice.

"I already have. Every beautiful thing here is layered over something broken. I'm tired of pretending I don't see it." I sense him behind me. "Come with me, Lane. You could get your old job back. We could . . . explore whatever this is between us."

Before I can respond, he spins me around, pulls me close, and crushes his mouth against mine.

I shove him away. "What're you doing, Briggs?"

His lips curl into that familiar dimpled smile, his voice low and confident. "We have chemistry, Lane. You feel it too. Don't pretend you haven't thought about kissing me."

I have—more than I care to admit. But not like this—not drunk, not desperate.

"I'm not going back to Richmond," I say, my tone leaving no room for argument.

His expression falters. "When did you decide that?"

I shrug. "Maybe I've known all along. Dad needs me. This town needs me. I'm not the kind of person who walks away." I meet his eyes, letting the words land. "I didn't think you were either."

Briggs's face hardens. "Maybe you don't know me as well as you think. I don't need you lecturing me about loyalty, Lane. Not tonight."

Turning away, he grabs the Maker's Mark bottle from the counter, unscrews it, and takes a long pull.

Something tightens in my chest, but I keep my voice steady. "Right. Not tonight. You're too busy running away. Good luck in Richmond, Briggs." I stride toward the door, letting myself out without looking back.

When I pull away from the curb, I catch him in the doorway—standing rigid, holding himself together like he's the one who deserves sympathy.

The irritation comes fast and unwelcome. I fix my eyes on the road. I'm done for tonight. He made his choice.

As I cross the bridge, I touch my fingers to my bruised lips. *We have chemistry, Lane. You feel it too.*

Of course I feel it. The pull between us has been simmering for weeks. But what just happened back there? That wasn't Briggs. Not the real him. Not the man who holds doors, watches his words, and respects boundaries.

Tonight was whiskey, wounded pride, and grief talking. And I'm not signing up for that. I just crawled out of a marriage to a man whose ego and infidelity scorched everything in its path. The last thing I need is another storm of male drama knocking me sideways. Briggs can sort himself out—or not. Either way, I'm not carrying the weight for him.

Needing to clear my head, I swing through town on my way

home. The square is eerily quiet, the kind of quiet that makes you feel like you've shown up after the credits roll. The dueling protest lines outside the courthouse are gone—*Free Clay, Justice for Addie* vanished.

Have they given up on Addie? On justice? On this town?

It's Halloween, and I expect to see costumed kids running around the square, collecting candy from shop owners. But the boutiques and restaurants are dark, their *Closed* signs flipped like they gave up hours ago.

What the heck is going on?

Then I see them—a line of black pickup trucks lined along the curb like a barricade. Men sit inside, silhouettes behind tinted glass, engines rumbling low. I'm so busy taking in the oversized tires and gun racks that I don't notice the man stepping into the street until I'm practically on top of him.

I slam on the brakes. The Bronco screeches to a stop inches from him.

He doesn't flinch.

The man is massive—over six feet tall and broad-shouldered—making my Bronco feel like a toy. He's wearing dark sunglasses, a ball cap yanked low, and a camo gaiter pulled up to his nose.

This isn't a costume.

There's nothing playful about the way he's blocking my path.

I throw the Bronco in park and jump out, my hand instinctively brushing the grip of my Glock holstered at my right hip. "Are you out of your mind? I almost ran you over."

His gaze moves over me with practiced indifference, like I'm an item on a checklist. "State your purpose, ma'am."

I narrow my eyes. "My purpose? What do you mean?"

"Your reason for being out past curfew. The town's in lockdown. The demonstrations got outta hand earlier. We hauled two loads to the station in the prisoner bus."

I flash my badge. "Here's my purpose. Where's yours?"

He jerks his thumb toward the row of idling trucks. "No credentials. We're not on the payroll. We're special ops—coordinating with the sheriff's department to keep the peace."

I stare at him, incredulous. "Special ops? In Tidewell?"

He scrolls a finger down his phone's screen. "What's your name?"

I arch a brow. "What's yours?"

"I asked you first," he says, voice smooth as cold steel. "I need to check if you're authorized to be out here."

"I don't need your authorization," I snap. "I'm a criminal investigator."

He removes his sunglasses slowly, like he's gifting me the privilege. Dead eyes—pits of polished obsidian—stare back at me. "You're Lane Sutherlin."

Fear tries to rise in me, but I shove it down. I learned a long time ago—too young—that fear is a weakness predators smell before you even feel it. I've spent my life learning how not to give it to them.

I straighten my spine. He picked the wrong woman to intimidate. "I am. And you are?"

"Colter Craddock." He steps closer, close enough to smell the faint mix of mint gum and gun oil clinging to his leather coat. A black-and-white patch is stitched to the chest—a raven perched on a crescent moon with wings spread like it's about to launch. *Night Ryders* curves beneath it in jagged block letters.

So this is the group of punks Judd warned me about—the self-appointed patrol claiming they're keeping Tidewell safe. Night Riders, spelled with a *y*. Cute.

I bark out a laugh. "What are the Night Ryders? Tidewell's own bargain-bin militia?"

"Watch yourself, little lady. You don't know who you're dealing with." He draws himself to his full height, imposing. I force myself not to retreat—not an inch. I meet those dead, obsidian eyes and lift my chin. I've been scared before—at the hands of another Craddock, no less. Is Wylie his father? The resemblance is enough to sour my stomach.

I give him a slow smile. "I've handled bigger threats than you, sweetheart. From your own family tree."

That gets him. A tiny flicker—jaw tightening, nostrils flaring—blink and you'd miss it. But I don't. He takes one step back, and the trucks behind him go silent.

I walk backward to my Bronco without breaking eye contact, climb in, and pull away. Only when I reach the end of the block do my hands start to shake.

That wasn't some local-boys-playing-soldier nonsense. This is what power looks like when it stops pretending to care about right and wrong.

Whatever this is—whatever he is—it's bigger than Clay, bigger than Addie, bigger than one bad verdict. Tidewell didn't just tilt off-balance tonight. It crossed a line.

And once a line like that is crossed, there's no going back.

Chapter Four

The encounter with Colter Craddock haunts me all night as I drift in and out of shallow sleep. Every time I close my eyes, I see those dead-black pits staring me down in the middle of Main Street. I finally doze off sometime around two. When I wake a few minutes before nine, sunlight is already peeking through the wooden blinds.

Scout is curled beside me, snoring softly, her paw draped over my leg like she's the one standing guard. I pull her closer, burying my face in her neck. She smells like warm fur and marsh air, faintly briny and unmistakably dog—comforting in a way nothing else is.

She's courage in canine form.

I lie there a minute, staring at the ceiling, contemplating the day ahead. Dad's caregiver asked for the day off to go to her son's football playoff game, which means it's just Dad and me until bedtime. I wish I could say I had a plan. I don't.

I can't remember the last weekend I wasn't chasing a lead, staking out a suspect, or filing reports. Even off the clock in Richmond, I was never really off.

And these past two months in Tidewell? Forget it. Morning, noon, and miserable sleepless nights—I poured everything I had into putting Clay Dalton behind bars. Now that the case is over, the town's a tinderbox, and apparently, we have Night Ryders enforcing curfew like Tidewell has become some third-world outpost.

I rub my eyes and sit up. I should get moving. Dad will be awake soon, and he doesn't do well on unstructured days.

If I'm being honest, neither do I. Too much stillness leaves room for thoughts I'd rather not revisit—last night's confrontation, yesterday's verdict, and Clay walking free.

Scout lifts her head and paws at me, tail thumping. She's ready. I'm not sure I am. But the day isn't waiting for either of us —and neither is whatever Tidewell has become.

My heart skips a beat when I notice the green light on the alarm pad in the upstairs hall. Someone disarmed the system, and I slept straight through the chime. A hard knot forms in my throat as I hurry down the hall to Dad's room.

His bed is made. His room is neat. And he's nowhere in sight.

My pulse spikes as I take the stairs two at a time, bracing for the worst. Relief rushes through me when I hit the bottom. The rolling rack of sleigh bells is positioned beside the front door, and a soft murmur of voices drifts from the back of the house.

I enter the kitchen to find Dad at the stove, scrambling what appears to be a dozen eggs in a large skillet like he's hosting brunch for the governor again.

Judd stands at the counter, filling three glasses of orange juice. He looks up at me. "There you are. Five more minutes and I was sending out a search party."

"I can't believe I slept so late." I cover a yawn that feels like it stretches clear down to my toes. "What're your plans for the day?"

Judd grunts. "Moving the rest of our stuff over from the apartment Wanna help?"

My gaze bounces from Judd to Dad and back again. "I can't believe I'm actually saying this, but sure, Dad and I will help. Won't we, Dad?"

Dad stops stirring, the spatula going still. He gives me a blank, faraway look, like he has no idea what we're talking about. "Sure, Bug," he says at last. "Whatever you say."

I glance out the window at the table on the patio where Judd's wife usually enjoys her morning coffee. "Where's Brandy? Is she eating breakfast with us?"

"Nah. She's not feeling well." Judd glances over at Dad, making sure his back is turned, then mouths, *morning sickness.*

I flash him a discreet thumbs-up. He hasn't told Dad about the baby yet, and I'm not about to steal that moment from him.

Dad plates the eggs and takes them over to the table. I lean across the island toward Judd. "He seems good this morning."

Judd lifts a shoulder. "Except that he tried to pour lemon juice in the eggs." He opens a cabinet, grabs his travel mug. "I can call some friends to help us move if you have better things to do."

Better things to do would require having a life, I think. Instead, I say, "I don't mind. It'll give Dad something to focus on. Honestly, I could use the distraction myself."

He nods, the hard lines around his mouth softening. "Whatever your reason, I appreciate it. Brandy's terrified to lift a finger. She thinks doing anything strenuous will put the baby at risk."

"I don't blame her, considering how long it took to get pregnant." I pour myself a coffee. "Since the cottage is fully furnished, what do you plan to do with the rest of your stuff?"

"I rented a storage unit. We'll take our clothes to the cottage and store the rest for now." He pauses. "Wonder how long *for now* will be."

I study his face, but his expression has gone stone still. I can't tell if he's talking about Dad—or the dark forces tightening their grip on this town.

I don't tell him about my encounter with Colter Craddock until later, when we're wrestling furniture into the moving van.

Dad and Brandy are inside the apartment boxing up the kitchen, and we've just loaded the last large piece—his king-size mattress.

I collapse against the side of the truck. "I met Colter Craddock last night."

Judd goes still. "Please tell me you didn't piss him off," he says, glaring at me over the top of his sunglasses.

I bite my upper lip. "Let's just say the exchange was heated. He stepped out in front of my Bronco. I almost ran him over. If anyone should be pissed, it's me." I square my shoulders, tightening my ponytail. "Who is he anyway? Wylie Craddock's son?"

Judd shakes his head. "Not Wylie. His older brother. Colt."

"I didn't know Wylie had an older brother." I shrug. "Then again, Wylie is four years older than me—Tommy's age. I wasn't exactly running in their circles."

"Colt and Colter are the fifth and sixth generations of Colt Craddocks—all of them mean sons of bitches. And Colter's the meanest of the lot." Judd looks at me hard. "Folks call him Colter for a reason. He's like the blade on a plow—cuts deep and leaves a line you can't rub out."

A shiver passes through me as I remember Colter's dead eyes. "His Night Ryders shut down the entire town last night. No trick-or-treaters. All the shops and restaurants closed."

Judd nods. "Busted a bunch of protestors too. I hear some of them are still in jail."

I shake my head in disbelief. "They call themselves special ops. Colter said they're coordinating with the sheriff's department to keep the peace. He admitted they're not employed by the Commonwealth of Virginia. Boone never should've allowed this."

Judd snorts. "Boone's a patsy, Lane. The Old Guard has ten miles of dirt on him. He'll do whatever they ask—kissing their asses while thanking them for the privilege."

I think back nineteen years. I have my own dirt on Boone. The question is, am I willing to light that match?

Judd kicks at some gravel on the road. "The trial's over, Lane. Now's the perfect time for you to leave town. Go back to Richmond. Brandy and I can take care of Dad. We'll hire full-time caregivers if necessary."

I toss up my hands. "Ugh. Not this again. I told you last night —I'm staying."

"And I'm asking you to reconsider." His voice drops. "The people controlling this town—guys like Wylie Craddock and Clay Dalton and Tate Vernon—are dangerous. If you stay, you'll get caught in their crossfire."

"I have to stay, Judd." I shake my head. "I can't explain why. It's just something I need to do."

I turn back toward the apartment. *Because leaving once already cost me too much.*

Judd catches up with me, spinning me around. "Try, Lane. Help me understand why you'd risk your life for a town that hasn't been your home in a decade."

"We may outgrow our hometowns," I say quietly, "but we never stop loving the people who shaped us."

"But why does it have to be you?" His voice breaks. "Let someone else do the dirty work. I already lost one sibling. I don't want to lose you too."

I hesitate, then shake my head. "Something happened to me a long time ago. I thought I could outrun it. Pretend it didn't matter." I meet his eyes. "But it did. And it still does."

"What're you talking about, Lane? What happened to you?"

I look away. "Forget I said anything."

I turn and walk back toward the apartment, leaving him standing there.

I've never spoken about what happened that night, nineteen years ago—not to Judd, not to Addie, not to anyone. But something has been shifting in me since I came home two months ago. The fog has finally lifted, and I can see things clear as day.

Every major decision I've made since I was fourteen traces back to that night.

I'm a thirty-five-year-old divorcée with no career and no hope of starting a family anytime soon. If I don't face this thing now— here, where it began—I never will.

Chapter Five

Dad and I spend the rainy Sunday working a jigsaw puzzle, pieces scattered across the old pine table like bits of a life we're still trying to put back together. His mind drifts into the past, and I'm content to let him go there. Every few minutes he'll tap a piece into place, then launch into a story I've heard a dozen times—fishing with Tommy at Catfish Point, our annual New Year's oyster roast, the year he argued a case all the way to the state supreme court.

As the rhythm of his voice rolls over me, I'm carried back to the carefree days of my youth, when everything was simple and safe. When I still had an older brother who made me laugh and a mother whose love once steadied me with a single touch. When Tidewell felt like a place that held me, not one that threatened to swallow me whole.

I glance at Dad—older now, thinner, fading in ways that hurt to admit—and something in my chest tightens. I want to make this town safe again. Not just for me—for him. For Brandy and Judd and their unborn child. For all of us.

This place shaped me, broke me, and called me home again. And now, whether or not I'm ready, it's asking something of me— something bigger than a badge, a rank, or the sheriff's approval.

It's asking me to save its soul from the kind of evil that wears a familiar face.

How can I possibly walk away?

I'm ready to roll Monday morning, downing coffee and chomping at the bit when Dad's caregiver arrives. I'm halfway down the drive when I realize I forgot something. I swing back toward the house, dart inside, and head straight to Dad's gun safe where we keep our valuables. I slide a thick manila envelope off the top shelf, tucked behind my firearms. A hunch tells me I might need this today.

Twenty minutes later, I step into the sheriff's department to find a uniformed Clay Dalton surrounded by his fellow deputies, basking in the glow of his acquittal. The Prince of Tidewell is back on his throne. In any other department, he'd be sidelined pending review. In Tidewell, the rules bend for their favorites.

If I wasn't sure about my decision before, I am now.

This is not my house. These are not my people.

I skirt the cluster of fawning deputies. No one stops me, no one asks for my badge. I'm halfway down the hall to Boone's office when Brody Talcott catches up with me. He's the only good cop on the force. He played a valuable role in saving Ben's life when someone tried to kill him while he was in jail.

"Hey, Lane." He moves to hug me, then settles for an awkward wave. "I'm glad to see you. Are you back on duty?"

I give him a sad smile. "Unfortunately, I'm turning in my badge. I can't be a part of this corruption anymore."

He hangs his head. "I've been thinking the same thing. The problem is, I don't know where I'd go. My dad's sick with cancer, and I need to stay close by to help my mom."

I clap his shoulder. "Then you stay right here. I'm off the force —but not the case. I need someone inside the sheriff's department I can trust."

"I guess I can stay a little longer. At least until Dad's . . . you know."

I give him a quick hug, pressing my cheek against his. "My dad's sick too. Alzheimer's. I know what you're going through. Hang in there."

"I will," he says with a shaky breath.

Pushing away, I continue down the hall to Boone's office. He's reclined in his chair, hands resting on his ample gut, feet kicked up beside a half-eaten jelly doughnut.

I clap once—sharp, loud.

He jolts upright so hard his chair squeaks. "Geez, Sutherlin!" His face goes red as a brake light. "You nearly gave me a heart attack. What're you doing here?"

I drop into the chair opposite him, crossing my legs like I own the place. "Just checking in. You didn't waste any time reinstating Clay."

Boone scoffs, waving a hand like I'm complaining about the weather. "Why wouldn't I? The jury came back not guilty. End of story."

"That's not how this works," I say.

He bangs his fist on his desk. "That's exactly how it works when there's no conviction. Internal Affairs reviewed it. The Commonwealth didn't file anything. No policy violation I can hang my hat on."

"I don't believe you. Internal Affairs doesn't clear murder cases overnight."

Boone shrugs. "They did."

I hold his gaze. "Because someone leaned on them."

I don't give him a chance to respond. "By the way, I had a little encounter with Colter Craddock and the Night Ryders over the weekend." I tilt my head. "I didn't realize you were outsourcing your law enforcement now."

"I . . . um . . ." His face mottles as he scrambles for words. "Let's just say they're on a special mission."

"Right. To restore peace." I let out a soft laugh. "Funny thing is, they seem to be the ones lighting the match under this powder keg."

"That's none of your business, Sutherlin."

"So, you're not paying them . . ." I tap my chin. "Which means they're either acting out of civic pride—or the Old Guard is bankrolling them." I lean forward. "Either way, someone other than you is calling the shots around here."

His jaw tightens. "Watch yourself, Sutherlin."

I smile. "I always do, Boone."

I reach into my pocket, pull out my badge, and set it on his desk with a soft metallic click. His eyes widen—not with authority but with surprise.

"I'm saving you the paperwork," I say. "I'm done pretending this department still answers to the law."

A flush creeps up his neck. "Good. You going back to Richmond, where you belong?"

"Not yet. Maybe never." I let the words hang. "I didn't realize how much I missed living near the water."

I stand, leaning across his desk just enough to make him uncomfortable. "I've got an old score to settle." I tap the badge with one finger. "Remember, Boone?"

He swallows hard, his Adam's apple bobbing.

"And while I'm at it," I add quietly, "I think I'll clean up this town a bit. Starting with the trash you've let pile up."

He snatches the badge off his desk. "You're on your own, Sutherlin."

"Oh, I know." I let the words settle before I continue. "I've been on my own for nineteen years. You made certain of that."

And then I walk out.

When I pass through reception, Clay's fan club is still huddled in the same spot. He glares at me, and I give him the one-finger salute.

A blast of November air sobers me on the way out. Boone knows I'm not backing down now. Maybe I just signed my own death warrant. I know the risks. I accept it anyway.

I pull onto the road and don't look back. I've spent nineteen years outrunning the past. It's time to face it before it takes everything else with it.

On my way out of town, I call an old friend at Richmond PD.

Amanda picks up right away. "Lane! I've been meaning to call you. I heard about Clay's acquittal. I'm so sorry."

I tighten my grip on the steering wheel as frustration crawls across my skin. "Thanks. I still can't believe a jury of twelve found him innocent."

"That's the system for you. I heard you aren't coming back. Please tell me it's not true."

"It's true," I say, explaining Dad's failing health.

"So what are you doing for work?" Amanda asks. "Are you still with the sheriff's department?"

"Nope. I'm doing some independent investigative work now. Which is actually why I'm calling." I keep my tone casual. "What's the status on the Ellison murder case?"

"What case?" Amanda says in a sarcastic tone. "Milo ruled her death a random home invasion."

"That's absurd. Random doesn't usually involve someone breaking into a doctor's office, wiping her entire database, and stealing every patient file she had."

"You're preaching to the choir, but I don't make the calls. After you left, Morales put Milo in charge. He closed the case fast." Amanda pauses. "Remind me—what was your connection to Ellison?"

"Addie was one of her patients," I say. "And I have reason to believe Ellison was involved in more than routine fertility treatments. She consulted out of her private office. Do you know where she actually performed procedures?"

"Hmm." Amanda thinks for a beat. "She worked out of a clinic with two other fertility specialists. I don't know the name, but it's near Henrico Doctors Hospital."

That's enough. "Thanks, Amanda. I owe you one. We'll talk soon."

I end the call.

When I stop for gas, a quick Google search tells me there are only two fertility clinics in Richmond—one downtown near VCU and Willow Creek Fertility Center near Henrico Doctors Hospital.

I spend the rest of the ninety-minute drive contemplating my approach. I'm not working the case in any official capacity. Even with the evidence in the manila envelope, I can't just walk in and start firing questions.

The Willow Creek complex comprises two identical but separate one-story brick buildings with signs pointing patients to the one on the left.

When I enter the clinic, I'm relieved to see Chloe Morgan, one of Dr. Ellison's nurses, seated behind the desk—same blonde braids, same earnest face. The bright, sterile lobby around her hums with nervous energy—a couple whispering in the corner, a phone ringing off the hook somewhere in the back.

She looks up from her computer, surprised to see me. "Detective Sutherlin. This is a surprise."

I smile softly. "Hey, Chloe. Good to see you. Are you working here now?"

"Yes." She quickly clicks out of whatever chart she was viewing. "They transferred some of Ellison's staff over. I assume you're not here for an appointment."

I chuckle. "No, not today. I'm tying up some loose ends on Ellison's case."

Chloe glances around, making certain no one is in earshot, and lowers her voice. "I was actually thinking about calling you. Some strange things are happening around here." She checks her phone for the time. "My lunch break is in ten minutes. Should we meet somewhere to talk?"

"Sure," I say. "The Chipotle is near your office."

She nods quickly. "I know it well. I'll see you soon."

I drive straight to Chipotle and wait for her just inside the door. We order our food and find a table for two.

I shake my burrito bowl and remove the lid. "So what's going on? Tell me about these strange things."

"Hang on." She takes several large bites of her burrito, holding up a finger while she finishes chewing. "Sorry. I'm starving." She sets down the burrito and wipes her mouth.

"So, you already know someone wiped Ellison's servers clean at her office and stole all her personal files. Well, some of the patient charts from the clinic are missing too. There may be others—we haven't completed a full inventory yet. Patients are furious." She leans in, voice dropping. "To make matters worse, their frozen eggs are gone."

That gets my attention. "Gone?"

"Vanished," she says. "From cryostorage."

"Where is cryostorage kept?"

Chloe hesitates. "In the lab, the identical building beside the clinic."

None of this surprises me. Addie's spreadsheets already painted a similar picture. But hearing confirmation sends a cold clarity through me. This is bigger than Ellison. Bigger than the clinic.

I keep my expression neutral, playing dumb to see how much she knows. "Are you saying someone stole them?"

Tears pool in her eyes. "I think so, yes. I assume they sold them—however sick that is."

"That's not just theft," I say quietly. "We're talking about human trafficking, Chloe."

She bobs her head, braids bouncing against her shoulders. "Yep. The other doctors are freaking out. We're getting calls from lawyers. Milo told us not to talk."

I hold up a hand. "Wait. Why would Milo tell you not to talk?"

She shrugs, sucking her tea through a straw like her life depends on it. "He says he's investigating, but I haven't seen him in six weeks—since the day of Dr. Ellison's . . ." She trails off, then swallows. "Since the day she died."

"Do you have any idea why some eggs were stolen and others weren't?"

Chloe nods, twisting her napkin. "The stolen eggs belong to high-profile patients."

A chill prickles down my spine. I set my fork aside. "Define high-profile?"

"Wealthy clients," she says, her voice dropping to a whisper. "Wives and daughters of politicians. Big donors. People with influence." She looks away. "We call them the beautiful people—money, power, prestige. Some have special talents. Others have husbands in very important positions. All are highly intelligent."

A cold wave rolls through me. Of course. Higher-quality eggs bring higher prices.

It hits me like a punch to the gut—the ugliness of it, bartering the most intimate part of a woman, her future children, her DNA, her very genes, like a commodity. My stomach knots, but my mind keeps moving, fitting the pieces together.

Chloe wipes her eyes and pushes her tray away. "I shouldn't have said anything."

"You absolutely did the right thing," I tell her. "And now you let me handle the rest."

She exhales, shaky, shoulders dropping a fraction.

I grab my jacket. "If anything else strange happens, you call me. Day or night."

Her eyes meet mine, wide and worried. "Be careful, Detective."

"You too, Chloe. You've wandered into a hornet's nest." I offer her a small smile. "But I've got your back."

She nods, grateful.

I pull my jacket on and step out into the cold air, my mind already on Morales.

Chapter Six

I don't tell my old boss I'm coming. I'm not sure how Sergeant Morales will respond to my sudden reappearance—whether he's ticked off that I resigned from Richmond PD or whether he understands my commitment to my family. My vote is the latter, and he doesn't disappoint. When he sees me standing in the doorway, he actually gets up from his desk and hugs me.

After a long minute, he pushes back, holding me at arm's length while he studies me. "You look good, Sutherlin. You've put on some weight. But the haunted look in your eyes is still there."

I now know the look he's talking about has more to do with my past troubles than my divorce. "I'm working on it."

"I understand. These things take time." He drops his hands from my shoulders. "Are you here on business? Or did you just miss me?"

"Both." I nod toward the door. "Better close that."

Morales sucks in a deep breath. "Here we go again. Why does trouble follow you like a rain cloud that hates sunshine?"

I chuckle. "Trust me, if I knew, I'd stop it."

He gestures at the empty chair across from his desk. "Have a seat. Tell me what's going on."

I lower myself into the chair. "How much do you know about Margaret Ellison's death?"

"Margaret Ellison," he says, confusion spreading across his face, as though searching his memory. "Oh." His head jerks up. "Dr. Ellison—the fertility specialist. She was killed during a random home invasion. Milo closed the case, claiming there was nothing more to it."

My jaw drops. "He closed the case? The same night of her murder, someone broke into her office, wiped her entire database, and walked off with every patient file she had. Sounds like there's a hell of a lot more to it to me."

His brows knit. "Hold on. I never heard about a break-in at her office."

Of course he didn't. Milo's fingerprints are all over that cover-up.

"In that case, let me fill you in." I walk him through everything I know—Ellison's death, the break-in at her private office, and my connection to her nurse. "Chloe's now working at the clinic Ellison shared with two other doctors—Willow Creek Fertility Clinic. Not only are patient files missing from the clinic, the harvested eggs belonging to those patients have vanished too."

Morales lets out a low whistle. "Egg trafficking. That's a new one for me. It's not like Milo to let something like this slide."

I lean forward. "He did more than let it slide, Sarge. According to Chloe, the other docs in the clinic are already getting calls from lawyers. Milo told them not to talk. He claims he's investigating, but she hasn't seen him since the day Ellison died."

Lines appear on his forehead. "Are you suggesting Milo's looking the other way?"

I proceed with caution. Milo is Morales's pet. "I'm not sure yet. But it seems like it to me." I pull the manila envelope out of my jacket, remove the stapled spreadsheets, and hand them to Sarge.

He slides on his readers and skims the pages. After a beat, he peers at me over the top of his glasses. "Where'd you get this?"

"Addie's mother found the digital version of those files on a thumb drive hidden in Addie's closet a few days after Ellison's murder. Confused about what they were, she passed them on to me. I have reason to believe Addie's husband is involved in some shady business dealings." I tap the papers. "What if Addie started digging—and whatever she uncovered got her killed?"

He gives me a grim look. "I'm sorry about Addie, by the way. I know you two were close. I followed the case. Seemed pretty airtight to me. I was surprised the jury acquitted." He taps the stack again. "Why didn't you turn this over as evidence?"

Morales knows we didn't present the file as evidence—which tells me he was paying close attention to the trial. Because of my association with the victim? Or because he's naturally curious about big cases?

"Tate fast-tracked the trial. We didn't have the time—or the jurisdiction—to investigate a possible egg trafficking ring. Without corroboration, it would've blown back on us."

"And how does Milo fit into all this?" he asks.

I sit back in my chair. "I honestly don't know. But he has connections in Tidewell. Clay somehow found out about my involuntary leave of absence from RPD. He claims you told him."

A crimson flush crawls up Morales's neck. "I've never spoken to Clay Dalton. But I know his family's part of the Old Guard."

I raise an eyebrow. "You know about the Old Guard?"

"I've heard the name passed around. Old-monied families with too much power and not enough ethics. Let's just say—their tentacles are long." Morales goes quiet, and I can almost hear the wheels spinning. "You still working for Boone?"

I shake my head. "Not as of this morning. There's a lot of bad stuff going down in Tidewell. And Boone appears to be right in the middle of it."

His eyes meet mine. "And you feel it's your civic duty to do something about it?"

I hunch a shoulder. "I can't turn my back on my hometown."

"And what do you want from me?"

I choose my words carefully. "I came here for information about the Ellison case. But it's clear you and I have the same . . ." I hesitate, then give a faint smile. "What did you call it? Trouble?"

"Trouble. Right. We're both getting drenched by the same rain cloud." Mischief tugs at his lips. "Might as well share an umbrella."

A smile parts my lips. "I'm listening."

Morales steeples his fingers under his chin. "I have a hard time believing it, but *if* Milo is operating on the wrong side of the law, I need to know about it." He pauses. "What you're poking at is bigger than Tidewell. If we work this from two sides, we might actually crack it."

"But how, sir? Tidewell is out of your jurisdiction."

"But the Willow Creek Fertility Clinic is located in Richmond —which means the egg trafficking is happening *in* my jurisdiction." He leans in, folding his arms on the desk. "You won't last long running solo against Boone and Tate. But if I bring you on board as a temporary investigator, you'll have access to certain records, permission to investigate Ellison's death on Richmond turf, and credentials."

My eyes widen. "You can do that?"

"Yes. Think of it as a temporary task force—limited scope, limited authority. You'd be operating as a consultant."

A badge—even one with limited credentials—stirs something in me I didn't expect. Maybe confidence. Maybe purpose. And Morales is solid. If I'm walking into a storm, I could do a lot worse than having him at my back.

"And no one else will know about this?" I ask.

He holds up three fingers. "Scout's honor."

Morales was an Eagle Scout. He doesn't make promises lightly.

I extend my hand across his desk. "Then we have a deal."

"Deal," Morales says, taking my hand and pressing the badge into my palm.

He pushes up from his chair. "I'll get us some coffee. We have some things to sort out. It might take a while."

He disappears down the hallway, and for a moment I let the room settle around me—the old desk scarred from years of elbows and paperwork, the bulletin board crowded with cases he'll never admit keep him up at night. When he returns, he hands me a steaming mug and settles in opposite me.

We spend the next hour going over everything. I take him through the break-in at Ellison's office, Chloe's account of the missing eggs, Addie's thumb drive, Clay's threats, the Night Ryders, and Boone's increasingly erratic behavior. Every time I think I've shocked him enough, something else pushes his brows a little higher.

When I finally finish, Morales leans back and lets out a long breath. "Damn, Lane."

"I know."

He stares down into his coffee for a moment, swirling what's left. "I've always liked that little town of yours. Reminds me of places my dad used to take me camping—small, friendly, tight-knit." He lifts his gaze to mine. "It'd be a crying shame to see it fall into the hands of a mafia-style outfit with too much money and not enough conscience."

"Right? My brother and his wife are expecting their first baby. That kid deserves to have the same safe place to grow up that we did."

"Agreed." Morales sets his mug down with a soft clink. "Whatever's happening in Tidewell is not small, Lane. And it's not stopping on its own."

"Trust me, I feel it. Down to my bones."

He studies me for a long moment, the lines around his eyes deepening. "Be smart. Be careful. And don't try to play hero. The Old Guard doesn't just fight dirty—they write the rules."

I stand to go. "I'm not looking to be a hero, Sarge. I just want justice."

He snorts. "In my experience, that's how heroes get made."

We walk to the door together. He stops with his hand on the frame, giving me one last look. "Remember, Lane. Storms don't care how prepared you think you are."

"I know," I say softly. "But I'm done running from this one."

I step out into the hallway, the badge a reassuring weight in my pocket. For the first time in years, the path ahead feels clear—even if it leads straight into the storm hovering over Tidewell.

Chapter Seven

He's back—the man who's been shadowing me off and on for the past six weeks.

He drives a late-model black Chevy Impala. So far, I've only caught glimpses—always at a distance, always disappearing before I could get more than the basics. Mid-forties, dark mustache, baseball cap pulled low.

I haven't seen him since before the trial. But today, he doesn't bother hiding. He's close enough to kiss my bumper as I exit the interstate and roll through West Point.

So the Old Guard knows I went to Richmond today. Did Shadow Man follow me to the clinic? To Richmond PD?

As I approach Tidewell's town limits, I crank the wheel and make a hard right into Oyster Bay Estates, giving him the one-finger salute when he shoots past. My mother lives in the gated community. Why she gave me a windshield sticker is anyone's guess—she certainly wasn't expecting a visit. Maybe she assumed I'd be on standby for dog duty while she vacationed somewhere expensive with my stepfather, Larry. Either way, it gets me through the gate.

I wind aimlessly along manicured streets, careful to avoid

Mom's. By the time I exit the impressive iron gates fifteen minutes later, the Chevy is nowhere in sight.

I glance at the dashboard clock. It's after five, but I'm too on edge to go straight home.

As I cross the bridge into town, I call Judd on Bluetooth. He answers on the second ring. "Hey. I had to go to Richmond today on business. And no, I'm not going back to my old job." I stop at a red light at the main intersection. "I'm just checking in. Are you with Dad?"

"Yep. Shawna left a few minutes ago."

I turn right on red, heading toward the waterfront. "Do you mind if I stop in town?"

"Nope. Take your time. Dad and I are out for a walk with Scout. We were just discussing dinner. How does jambalaya sound?"

I groan. "Delicious. Keep this up, and I'll gain ten pounds."

He chuckles. "You could stand to put on a few."

"I'll be home in an hour. Let me know if you need anything from the market," I say, then hang up.

Slip 99 is almost always packed—breakfast until closing at midnight. But today, only two tables are occupied, and the bar sits empty.

Instead of taking my usual stool by the window, I choose one closer to the door, at the end of the bar where it makes a forty-five-degree turn toward the back. From here, I have a clear line of sight to the entrance in case Shadow Man shows up.

Frankie tosses a napkin in front of me. "Hey, Lane. What can I get you? The usual?"

I nod. "Minus the oysters."

She pours tequila and soda over ice, drops in a lime wedge, and slides the glass across the bar.

"Where's Cooter?" I ask, sipping the drink.

He's the main reason I'm here. Cooter has his finger on Tidewell's pulse, and I'm curious what he's been hearing about the Night Ryders.

"He's taking the night off."

I frown. "Cooter? That's not like him. Is everything okay?"

She gestures toward the nearly empty dining room. "If you call this ghost town okay. He's taking advantage of what he hopes will be a short-lived lull to get some much-needed rest."

I lift the glass, pausing before I drink. "Is there a reason for this lull?" I ask, already suspecting her answer.

She lowers her voice, even though no one is within earshot. "The Night Ryders have the whole town running scared. No one dares leave home after dark."

Anger flares. Innocent people holed up in their homes because a few control-hungry cowards want to play war games in the dark.

The door bangs open, and I tense, expecting Shadow Man to slither in. Instead, a man I've never seen before steps inside—one I definitely would've remembered. And damn, he's attractive.

He's older—forties, maybe—too old for me, but who cares? I can look. His hair is thick and black, brushed back carelessly, like he ran a hand through it on his way inside. Expensive in that understated outdoorsman way—waxed coat, tailored corduroys, leather boots broken in just enough to look authentic.

He takes the stool at the bend in the bar—making it impossible not to look at him.

So the stranger wants to flirt. I suppose there are worse crimes.

He settles into his seat with a satisfied sigh. "Ah, yes. Just what I need—a pretty woman to look at while I eat." He reaches for a menu without taking his eyes off me. "Care to share an appetizer?"

"With a total stranger?" I say, lifting my glass. "Hard pass."

His gaze drifts down the menu. "What about oysters? You can have your own shells."

"If I wanted oysters, I'd order them myself."

He grins like he thinks he's charming. "Come on now, don't play hard to get. We'll call this our first date."

"Ha. You're old enough to be my father."

He looks up from the menu, pinning me with a gaze so sharp it feels like a shove. His eyes are startling—clear and green, cold as a snake's. "Definitely not your father. Maybe your older brother."

Something in the way he says it turns my stomach. Like he knows my father. And he's not talking about Judd. He's talking about Tommy.

Before I can respond, Frankie bursts through the double doors with a tray of food. She skids to a stop when she sees him. Her lips part—ready to speak—but whatever she planned to say dies on the spot. She forces herself forward, pastes on a smile, and hustles toward the dining room, leaving the air colder behind her.

When I look back at the man, he's still watching me—eerie, like his thoughts have already crossed a line.

Before I can decide whether to look away or stare him down, a hand clamps around my upper arm. I whirl, ready to swing, expecting to see Shadow Man. To my surprise, it's Briggs.

He yanks me off my stool and hooks an arm around me, pulling me in so tight I think I might pop. "She's with me," Briggs says to the man in a voice that dares him to say otherwise.

The man's lip curls—something between amusement and annoyance. Those cold green eyes narrow, sizing Briggs up like a wolf assessing another alpha.

"Well now," he drawls, leaning back on his stool. "Didn't realize she was claimed."

"Claimed?" I snap, jerking free of Briggs's grip. "I'm not property, and no one owns me."

But Briggs doesn't back away. "Let's go," he says quietly. Not a command. Not a plea. A warning.

I let him take me by the hand and lead me to the door. The second we're out of sight of the bar, I wrench free, but Briggs doesn't slow until we're halfway across the parking lot.

"What the heck, Briggs?"

He doesn't flinch. "You're being followed, Lane."

My breath catches. "That's old news. Shadow Man's been on my tail for two months. I thought I told you about him."

"I'm not talking about him." He jerks his chin back toward the bar. "I mean *him.* You obviously don't know who that is."

I glance toward Slip 99, but it's too far to see through the windows. "Obviously. Should I?"

Briggs lets out a humorless snort. "Yeah. But I get why you might not. He's older, and you've been gone a long time. He's Colt Craddock. Wylie Craddock's older brother."

The name worms down my spine, cold and paralyzing. "Colter Craddock's father?"

Briggs nods. "And his presence here tonight wasn't a coincidence. They're watching you, Lane. You've been marked."

I ease back into the shadows between parked cars, eyes darting and one hand sliding to the butt of my pistol. When I'm sure we're alone, I head quickly for my Bronco with Briggs at my heels.

We climb inside, and I crank the heat.

"Look," Briggs says, softer now. "I owe you an apology."

"For what?" I play dumb, like I don't already know, like his behavior the other night didn't unsettle me more than I care to admit.

"For being an ass the night of the verdict—for being out of line." He meets my eyes, holds my gaze, making me squirm. "I've had the weekend to think about it. I was drunk and angry. Not at you. At Tate and Clay and the whole damn circus. At what they're doing to our town. Honestly? I'm scared out of my mind."

I swallow hard, unsure what to do with the seriousness in his voice.

His shoulders rise and fall in a slow, steady breath. "I can't leave Tidewell. Not with the Old Guard circling like vultures. Not with guys like Craddock playing mafia lord."

"Briggs—"

"No," he cuts in. "Let me finish. I'm not letting this town get carved up by a bunch of power-hungry bastards. And I'm sure as hell not letting you fight them alone."

Silence settles between us, heavy and tense, full of things neither of us is ready to say.

"Let me follow you home," he says. "Just to make sure Shadow Man doesn't bring his friend along."

My pulse skips. I hate that part of me is relieved.

"Fine," I say flatly. "But don't expect a thank-you."

A ghost of a smile touches his mouth. "Wouldn't dream of it."

He reaches for the door handle, but I grab his arm. "Before you go, we need to clear the air. You tried to kiss me."

His eyes flick to my mouth. "Yeah. Bad timing. But I'm not sorry." He leans in, and for a heartbeat, I'm sure he's going to kiss me again. But his lips land softly on my cheek instead. "We need to stay focused. We can't let our emotions get in the way."

I nod. "Agreed."

His mouth hovers near my ear, his breath warm against my cheek. "But soon," he whispers. "And it'll be worth the wait."

He pulls back, gently lifting my chin with his fingers. "Meet me in the morning. Salty Bean at nine," he says, and then he's gone.

I sit there a second, breath caught somewhere between my ribs.

Shadow Man on one side.

Colt Craddock on the other.

And now Briggs in the middle.

Tomorrow, I stop being hunted. The real fight begins.

Chapter Eight

I take extra time with my hair and makeup on Tuesday morning. But my reflection makes me cringe. That woman, that stranger, looks like she's trying too hard—wearing armor instead of skin. I wash my face, start over, and keep it simple.

Briggs can take me as I am. I'm done bending myself into shapes that fit someone else's world.

When I walk into the Salty Bean Café thirty minutes later, Briggs is already there.

"Sorry, I'm late. I had to wait for Dad's caregiver." I slide onto the banquette beside him at the corner table by the window. "How do you always manage the best seat in the house?"

He chuckles. "I get here early. Today, I was waiting on the sidewalk out front when they opened."

The scattered papers in front of him confirm he's not kidding.

"Here." He nudges a coffee toward me. "I hope it's not cold."

I take a sip. "Lukewarm."

I tug off my coat and settle in.

His eyes roam my body, lingering at the cleavage peeking over the top of my flannel shirt. A soft smile touches his lips—the same lips that whispered *It'll be worth the wait* against my ear last night.

Heat creeps up my neck. I really need to rethink my wardrobe.

He waves a hand in front of my face. "Earth to Lane."

I force my attention away from his lips. "Sorry. Did you say something?"

"I asked if you brought Shadow Man along for the ride this morning?"

"Of course. He cruised past while I was parking. I'm sure he's idling around the corner as we speak." I reach over and pinch off a piece of his bagel. "By the way, thank you for last night. For saving me from Colt Craddock."

He rolls his eyes. "Glad I showed up when I did. You were seriously flirting with him."

I gasp, full fake indignation. "No, I wasn't."

But I had been. And it unsettles me more than I'm willing to admit.

"So . . ." He leans in closer. "Where are we?"

I fill him in—Boone, Richmond, Chloe, Morales.

Briggs blows out a breath when I finish. "I'm glad you're done with Boone. He claims he's one of the good guys, but he's been sucking up to the Old Guard so long he doesn't remember what *good* looks like." He rubs a palm over his jaw, still processing. "But I'll sleep easier knowing Morales is backing you. You need someone watching your six."

Then his gaze sharpens. "But the clinic . . ." He whistles. "Once those patients figure out their eggs are missing, they'll be all over that place like hornets on a busted nest."

I nod. "It's already started. I'm worried what will happen if the wrong people get spooked."

Briggs studies me. "You think those *wrong people* are the Old Guard?"

"Stands to reason. I'd bet my life that Clay is part of this. I can't imagine where else Addie could've gotten the spreadsheets."

Briggs snorts. "Clay may be involved, but he's not smart enough to mastermind something this big. Guys like Clay don't run operations. They take orders—and when things go sideways, they take the blame."

I hold his gaze. "I'm counting on it."

We sit in silence for a minute. I imagine arresting Clay again—this time with ironclad evidence that will send him away for life.

"So where do we go from here?" Briggs asks.

"I'll continue to dig into the egg trafficking. But the more urgent issue is jury tampering. Time is working against us. The further we get from the verdict, the colder that trail gets. Maybe we should ask your girlfriend to interview the jurors as a human-interest piece, to see what she can shake loose."

Briggs's eyebrow shoots up. "My girlfriend?"

I ball up my napkin and toss it at him. "Alex, you idiot. Stop pretending she doesn't have a crush on you."

He mutters something under his breath, ears going a little pink.

"Regardless, she's the perfect person to handle the project. She spent decades reporting on politics in DC. She can smell a cover-up before most people can spell it."

"I'll let you take the lead on this," Briggs says. "I need to keep my head down. Tate's already itching to fire me, and I'm a lot more useful to our cause as the commonwealth's attorney than I am without the title."

"That makes sense." As the black Chevy Impala passes by the window, an unwelcome thought presents itself. "There goes Shadow Man. Considering I'm target numero uno with the Old Guard—and they're watching my every move—you should probably not be seen with me."

His mouth pulls tight—he doesn't try to hide that he hates the idea. "You're probably right. At least for a while." A smile tugs at his lips. "We can still text. I'll FaceTime you late at night when you're in your pajamas."

I shoot him a look. "What happened to hands off for now—*it'll be worth the wait?*"

Mischief twinkles in his baby blue eyes. "We agreed to hands off, not eyes off."

I slam back the last of my cold coffee. "Focus, Briggs. We can't afford the distraction."

That wipes the smile off his lips. "You're right. Let's give Shadow Man—and anyone else watching—a show. We'll fake an argument. Outside. On the sidewalk. Make it look like you and I are no longer working together."

I smile. "That's brilliant."

He slides a stack of file folders across the table. "Here are my notes on all the jurors."

I take them, flipping through the tabs. "I'll jot down my thoughts and pass them on to Alex. I should probably meet with her in private," I add. "No sense putting a spotlight on her."

"Good call. Does that mean you're handing the project over to her?"

"Hmm." I pinch my chin, considering his question. "I think so. Alex is the only one who can get the jurors talking without raising alarms. If they see me coming, they'll shut down—or worse, tip off the Old Guard."

He exhales a breath of resignation. "Keep her on a short leash, Lane. Make sure she understands the lines—we can't afford anyone crossing them."

I salute him. "Ten-four."

"Do you think you can ditch Shadow Man?" Briggs asks, stuffing his folders and pads in his carrier bag.

I stare at him. "Did you seriously just ask me that?"

He palms his forehead. "What was I thinking, asking the fearless Detective Sutherlin such a ridiculous question?"

He stands, scooping up the empty coffee cups. "Ready?"

"Yep. We've got this. But let's make it convincing." I push back from the banquette and follow him out, my pulse ticking fast.

The moment the door swings shut behind us, his voice goes sharp. "I don't know what the hell you expect from me!"

Heads turn. Perfect.

"I expect you to act like you have a spine!" I snap back.

Briggs throws up his hands. "Unbelievable. Absolutely unbelievable!"

We walk in opposite directions, both fuming for show. Anyone watching wouldn't question a thing.

I keep my stride clipped and angry until I've rounded the corner, heading in the direction of the courthouse. Without glancing over my shoulder, I duck into the stylish women's boutique, Birdie & Belle.

The bell over the door jingles, soft and cheerful, wildly out of sync with the adrenaline buzzing under my skin. I hover near the display window just long enough to see Shadow Man's Impala creep past, slow as a shark fin slicing water.

I thumb off a text to Alex.

> Need help on a sensitive project. Can we meet?
> In private?

Little dots appear. Disappear. Appear again.

> Right up my alley. Can you come to my place?
> Just finished yoga. Need an hour.

> Perfect. Drop me a pin.

Hallie—the boutique's young owner—emerges from behind the counter, a bright splash of silk scarves draped over her arm.

"Hey there, Lane. Good to see you again." She pulls me into a warm embrace, scarves and all.

Hallie had been dating my older brother when he died in a boating accident. We were never friends—she and Tommy were four years ahead of me—but our shared grief pulled us into the same orbit after the funeral. Hallie and I reconnected last month, when Addie was still missing and I wandered into the boutique searching for anything—*anyone*—who might help me find her.

Finally, she steps back, smoothing a hand over the silk scarves.

"I've been thinking about you. About Tommy, too, actually. A lot lately."

My breath hitches. "Really?"

Hallie nods, eyes fixed on the scarves as she arranges them on a decorative iron rack. "I can't get him off my mind. I keep wondering what kind of man he would've become. His career . . . the woman he would've married." Her voice softens. "He was destined for greatness."

A lump rises in my throat so fast it nearly chokes me. "Yes," I say softly. "He was."

The silence stretches. I choose my words carefully. "I've been thinking a lot about the accident lately."

Her hands still.

"Where were you that day, Hallie?"

In one of Dad's recent delusional spells, he'd insisted a girl had been with Tommy the day of the accident. The claim made no sense—we've always been told Wylie Craddock was the only other passenger in the boat—but Dad had been unusually adamant. He hadn't sounded confused. He'd sounded certain. And now I can't stop wondering if the truth about that day slipped out when his guard was down.

Hallie drops the last scarf on the rack and turns to me. "I was on the beach with everyone else. Tommy was in a foul mood after he and Wylie got into that fight. I was actually relieved when he took off in his boat alone—I figured he needed some time by himself to calm down." She shakes her head. "He despised Wylie. I've never understood how they ended up in the boat together later that afternoon."

"Me either. That's one of many questions I have about the accident."

When the time is right, Hallie and I will sit down and compare notes. But not today—not with Shadow Man breathing down my neck.

Hallie spreads her arms wide. "What can I help you with? Are you looking for anything in particular?"

I glance around at the racks of stylish clothes. And since I have time to kill before my meeting with Alex . . . "Not really. My wardrobe could use a glow-up. Nothing fancy. I'm a jeans kinda girl."

"That's cool." Hallie spins me by the shoulders. "But you're wearing *Levi's*. You need designer denim to show off that nice butt. I'd kill for those curves."

"Designer sounds expensive," I say warily.

"Not necessarily." She leads me to a wall stacked with wooden cubbies filled with jeans. She gives me the once-over, assessing my size, and pulls several pairs from the right box.

Hallie herds me toward the dressing room. "Get in there," she says, shoving a stack of jeans into my arms. "And don't come out until you're a new woman."

I laugh and slip behind the curtain. I peel off my Levi's and tug on the first pair of designer jeans. They slide on like they were sewn for me. Soft. Forgiving. Sinful. I turn toward the full-length mirror—and freeze. Goodness. I've never noticed my butt before. Not bad.

Hallie's voice floats from outside. "How's the fit?"

I'm still staring, stunned. "You're right. The Levi's weren't doing me any favors."

She laughs. "Good. Try the next pair. I'm tossing in some sweaters."

A soft thump hits the bench as she drops a handful of cozy knits over the door. I swap jeans, pull on a cream turtleneck, and catch my reflection again. I actually look like a woman who has her life together.

I run a hand over my hip, turning slightly left, then right. *Would Briggs notice the change?* The thought comes uninvited, flickering through me like a warm ember.

I shake my head hard. *No distractions, Lane. Focus on the bad guys, not your butt.*

I pull on a second sweater—a cherry-red cashmere crewneck that makes my skin look warmer and healthier, like someone who slept eight hours and doesn't have a militia watching her every move.

By the time I plunk my credit card down on the counter, I've forgotten that I'm currently unemployed. Well . . . mostly unemployed—minus the modest stipend Morales is paying me for *consulting*. But I have savings, and when was the last time I bought anything that wasn't tactical or functional?

Hallie folds the sweaters in tissue paper. "These are perfect for you, Lane."

"I think so too. Thanks for your guidance." I clear my throat. "By the way, I'm working an undercover situation right now."

Hallie's eyes widen. "Oh?"

"Nothing dangerous. Nothing for you to worry about. I promise." I wouldn't be in the shop if my presence put Hallie—or anyone else—in harm's way. "But do you mind if I slip out your back door? I've got a tail, and I need to lose him."

She studies me a beat, then nods. "Of course. Come on."

Hallie reaches under the counter, grabs her keys, and leads me down a narrow hallway past the staff restroom. We stop at a faded blue door with a metal push bar. She leans in, her voice low. "If whoever is following you comes in, I'll tell them I never saw you."

I smile at her. "Thanks."

Hallie presses the bar, and the door clicks open into the alley. "Be careful, Lane."

I give her a grateful smile. "Always."

I slip out the back, letting the door ease shut behind me, and hurry down the alley toward the coffee shop where I parked my Bronco. Shadow Man is nowhere in sight.

Chapter Nine

Alex lives on the second floor of a converted warehouse in Tidewell's waterfront shopping district. The stairwell leading up from the antiques boutique below smells faintly of old wood and lemon polish.

She comes to the door in expensive champagne-colored loungewear—cashmere, I think—with her damp dark hair piled on top of her head in a messy knot. She's strikingly beautiful without a smudge of makeup on her flawless face. She exudes the kind of elegance that doesn't ask for attention—it assumes it.

"Thanks for meeting me on such short notice," I say.

"Of course." She opens the door wider, giving me room to enter. "I'm intrigued by your sensitive project."

The apartment's open floor plan offers exposed brick walls, high beams, and floor-to-ceiling windows overlooking the marina. I see none of the expected coastal fussiness here—no driftwood accents, no nautical accessories, no carefully curated charm. Soft touches from her life as a DC journalist are everywhere—a velvet sofa in deep burgundy, Oriental rugs, and books in every corner. Some are stacked horizontally on shelves, others piled in neat little towers beside the sofa, a few left open on the coffee table as if she stepped away mid-thought.

On one wall, a giant corkboard is cluttered with printed articles, handwritten notes, and a map of Tidewell peppered with colored thumbtacks. This is the home of a thinker. A lived-in workspace. A sanctuary. A war room.

In my next life, when my situation with Dad changes, I'd like to live in a place just like this.

"Can I get you something to drink?" Alex asks. "Coffee? Tea? Water?"

I shake my head. "I'm fine, thanks."

"Then have a seat." Alex motions me to the sofa. Besides the floor, there's nowhere else to sit.

I sink into the soft down cushions—a sofa I'd like to nap on. "The project involves interviewing the jurors from the Clay Dalton trial," I say, watching closely for her response.

Her dark eyes flash. "I was hoping you'd say that. I've been itching to get my hands on those jurors. I had a bad feeling about that trial from day one. Tate rushing the case. Jurors acting like they want to spit-polish Clay's shoes. And Travis Keene's last-minute 'family emergency,' " she says, hooking her fingers in air quotes.

"How much do you know about the alternate, Earl Minton?"

I watch carefully for her response. She doesn't blink. Of course she knows about Minton's son's DUI. She's sharp and personable—the kind of woman with friends in all the right places. And a few in the wrong ones too.

"Shouldn't I be asking *you* that?" she says finally.

I hold her gaze. "If we're gonna work together, Alex, we need to put all our cards on the table. No holding back."

She hesitates, as though choosing her words carefully. "I know that Minton owes Tate a very large favor, if that's what you're referring to."

"Right. So we're on the same page."

She grabs her iPad off the coffee table and falls back into the sofa cushions. "Of all the jurors, Travis Keene appeared the most willing to convict Clay. He could've been the one to hang the jury. Then—poof—family emergency, and he's gone."

"It doesn't smell right to me either." I nod for her to continue. "How would you approach the interviews?"

"I won't start with Travis. That would be too obvious." She taps her iPad screen. "A lot depends on who I can locate, but I'd prefer to ease in with a few women. They're usually quicker to loosen their tongues, especially if they think they're helping shape the narrative."

I tilt my head. "Meaning?"

Her lips part in a sly smile. "Meaning people love to talk if you make them feel important. I'll come in friendly, tell them I'm doing a human-interest piece on civic duty in small towns and would love to hear about their experience as a juror on the Clay Dalton trial." She shrugs. "Soft entry."

"And once they start talking?" I ask.

"Then I pivot. I'll hit them with tougher questions. *When did you decide Clay was innocent? Was there a moment that swayed you? Anyone on the panel stand out as a leader?* That sort of thing. People always reveal more than they intend when they have to reconstruct a moment."

I'm fascinated. I've never thought much about what goes into interviewing. "Will you do this through Facebook Live?"

Alex grins. "Of course. Recorded interviews choke people up. I'll catch them off guard—homes, workplaces, the grocery store. It feels casual. Gives them less time to rehearse. Live interviews turn people into performers. And performers always spill the most."

I'm impressed. Alex clearly knows what she's doing.

I rise from the sofa. "All right, then. Let's get started. Send me updates so I don't miss the interviews."

"I'll definitely stay in touch. But don't worry. If you miss the live feed, I'll post the clips on my page afterward."

I move toward the door. "By the way, Briggs gave me his files. I'll add my notes and get them to you as soon as possible."

Alex nods once. "I'd love to hear his—your—thoughts."

The pause is small, but I catch it. Whether by design or slip of the tongue, Alex doesn't consider my input essential. Suddenly ready to be anywhere but here, I step into the hallway, and the door closes softly behind me.

I hurry down the stairs, not slowing until I reach the boardwalk. Outside, the wind off the marina cuts sharp and cold, clearing my head. Though he's nowhere in sight, I sense Shadow Man nearby—watching and waiting. I climb into the Bronco and pull away from the curb before he shows himself, before the world complicates things again.

A strange feeling settles in my chest, unsettling and sharp. I'm homesick.

How can that be when I've only been gone from home a couple of hours? But the pull is unmistakable as I follow the familiar Tidewater Drive toward the farm.

I need to see Dad. Not because anything is wrong—at least, not more wrong than usual—but because his presence steadies me. Because when his mind slips, the house still remembers him. And Scout. Scout will be stretched out in her usual patch of sunlight spilling through the French doors in the family room, tail thumping when she hears my truck, reminding me that some things are simple and loyal and exactly where they're supposed to be.

I need the land too. The familiar curve of the driveway. The marsh smell. The way the wind moves through the trees like it's always done, indifferent to corruption and courtrooms and men who think they can manipulate outcomes from the shadows.

Out here in the real world, people posture. Perform. Measure each other.

At River Birch, things are what they seem.

For now, I'm going home—to the only place that still feels real.

Chapter Ten

The sight of Lally at the stove warms my heart and settles something in my chest—her back erect, white dress uniform, milk-coffee skin unwrinkled with age. She's been our housekeeper since I was a little girl—a mother to me when Roxie abandoned us. I've never seen her wear regular clothes except on rare occasions—at Tommy's funeral and when she drops in on her way home from church. She's family. And family is how I know I'm exactly where I need to be.

I peer over her shoulder at the bubbling pot, breathing in the rich aroma of basil and garlic. "Smells amazing. Is that your homemade tomato soup?"

She smiles without turning from the stove. "Mm-hmm. I used the tomatoes I put up last summer. And I've got grilled cheeses too—Gruyère, sharp white cheddar, and bacon. Just the way you like it."

I rub my hands together. "How much longer? Should I get Dad?"

She chuckles. "Sure. Lunch will be ready in five minutes."

As I pass through the family room, I spot Shawna in the chair by the window, tapping on her phone with one eye on Dad's study door down the hall. We pay her a lot of money to sit in that chair. But it's money well spent if it keeps Dad from wandering. This week alone, she's stopped him from slipping out of the house five times. And it's only Tuesday.

I hate how normal this is becoming—waiting for the next time he'll forget where he is, or worse, who I am.

I never know which version of Dad the hour will bring. Sometimes he's sharp as ever—the bright, witty judge who could cut a man to ribbons with one raised brow. Other times, he drifts, eyes unfocused, mind stuck somewhere I can't reach. And then there are times when he turns uncharacteristically mean.

And that's the version that sits down beside me at the breakfast counter. He jabs a thumb over his shoulder at Shawna. "Why is that woman always here?" he booms, loud enough for Shawna to hear in the adjacent room.

I press a finger to my lips. "Shh! Don't be rude, Dad. She's here to help us—to help you."

"Help me? All she does is sit in that chair and stare at her phone."

"Well . . ." I straighten, shifting on the barstool. "If you'd let her, she could take you for walks around the property. Or for long drives in the country. Or you could go on excursions into town, maybe get some ice cream."

"Ice cream," he snaps. "Stop condescending to me, Roxie. You make me sound like a toddler."

Roxie? The name hits like a slap. Dad's doctor warned us not to correct him when he's confused, but I draw the line at being mistaken for my mother.

"I'm Lane, Dad."

He scowls at me, defensive. "Of course you are. I may be forgetful, but I know my daughter."

I sink my teeth into the grilled cheese before my tongue gets me into trouble.

I'm savoring the mix of gooey cheeses when, to my horror, Dad lifts his soup bowl and noisily slurps up tomato soup, not bothering with a spoon.

I train my eyes on my plate, ignoring him as best I can. I need lessons from my brother in keeping cool at moments like this. I eat my lunch in silence while he mutters on about firing Shawna. By the time he wanders off to his study for a nap, my patience is scraped raw.

I settle in at the old farm table to go over Briggs's juror files. Warm afternoon sunlight spills through the window beside me, heavy enough to make my eyelids droop. I'm fading, elbow propped on the table, chin resting in my hand, laptop open beside me, when Alex pops up on the screen, snapping me fully awake.

She's annoyingly perfect in a black leather jacket and tailored jeans, exuding confidence as she stands with a middle-aged man in a golf pullover on a quiet suburban lawn.

"Welcome to *Tidewell Unfiltered*. I'm Alex Monroe, and today I have the pleasure of speaking with Tommy Griggs, a juror from the Clay Dalton trial."

I turn up the computer's volume. I give her credit—she doesn't waste any time. I'm only mildly irked that she didn't text me about the interview. And why is she interviewing a man when she wanted to start with the women?

Tommy lifts a hand, waving awkwardly at the camera. "Uh. Yeah. Hi."

Why is he sweating when it's fifty-two degrees outside?

Alex angles her body toward him. "Tommy, thanks for speaking with me. First question: How did it feel serving on such an important case?"

Tommy clears his throat. "Yeah . . . well . . . you know. It was . . . something."

Alex narrows her eyes. "Something good? Something stressful?"

"Oh—uh—just jury duty." He gives a weak laugh. "Nothing more to say, really."

Alex's smile doesn't budge. "Did anything about the deliberations stand out to you?"

Tommy's eyes dart to the camera like he wants to sprint off

frame. "Nope. Regular deliberations. Real standard." He swallows hard. "We followed the . . . uh . . . directions."

Alex nods slowly. "Did you feel any pressure? From other jurors? From . . . outside sources?"

Tommy freezes. Totally still. Then he clears his throat again—loud this time. "I-I should probably go. Got a client meeting in ten," he says, pointing at his watch.

Alex gently pushes. "Just one more question: When did you decide Clay Dalton was innocent?"

Tommy's jaw clenches. And then he shuts down completely. "No comment. Sorry. I can't—I shouldn't't've—yeah, I gotta go."

He hurries off camera so fast he nearly trips over his own front steps.

Alex, still composed, faces the camera. "Well, now, that was informative."

Informative indeed. Tommy Griggs is scared of something—something far more powerful than Alex's questions.

I return my attention to the juror files.

Thirty minutes later, Alex pops up on the screen again. This time she's on a tidy front porch beside sixty-one-year-old Carla Boone—retired schoolteacher, church volunteer, and distant cousin of Sheriff Boone.

Alex flashes her polished smile. "We continue our interviews with Carla Boone—juror number eight."

Carla wiggles her fingers at the camera, beaming like she's on *The Today Show.* "Hey, y'all."

Alex keeps her tone soft, warm, calculated. "Carla, thank you for speaking with me. First question: How did it feel serving on such a high-profile case?"

"Oh, honey, it was thrilling," Carla says, clasping her hands dramatically. "I mean, nobody wants someone to get murdered, of course, but it sure made jury duty more exciting than usual!"

I drag a hand over my face. *Oh, Lord.*

Carla barrels on. "And that Clay Dalton is just the sweetest boy. Always holds the door for me when I see him at the Piggly

Wiggly. Told me once at a church picnic that he liked my banana pudding. Such manners! That is not a man who kills his wife."

Alex's lips twitch, but her next words are gentle. "So you felt that way before the trial began?"

"Oh heavens, yes. Everybody in Tidewell knows Clay is good people."

"And during deliberations," Alex presses, "did anyone on the jury disagree with you?"

Carla leans conspiratorially toward the camera. "Well, we were supposed to keep all that private, but I don't see any harm in talking about it now that the trial's over."

Alex keeps her face perfectly neutral. *She's good.* "Tell me about your experience."

Carla rolls her eyes. "Travis Keene was the troublemaker."

A cold prickle runs down my spine.

Alex tilts her head. "Trouble how?"

"He was acting all high and mighty, saying we needed to 'respect the process and evaluate the evidence.' " She air quotes like the phrase physically offends her. "He kept insisting we take votes. But the rest of us already knew Clay was innocent. Then he bailed on deliberations because of his rumored family emergency."

Alex's expression falters a fraction. *"Rumored?"* she repeats softly.

Carla waves a dismissive hand. "Mm-hmm. The whole thing smelled fishy. But anyway . . . " She gives a bright smile to the camera. "Justice was served. Clay's a free man, thank the Lord."

Justice was definitely not served.

Alex signs off with a warm thank-you, but I barely hear it. Because Carla Boone didn't just talk. She detonated a landmine.

I'm still sitting dazed in my chair, replaying Carla's *Tidewell Unfiltered* interview for the umpteenth time when Alex calls.

I swipe to answer. "Great job, Alex! You just got Carla to confess to half a dozen violations of jury protocol . . . on camera . . . while smiling."

"Thanks. But, Lane, we've got a problem." Her tone is so serious she shuts me up mid-gloat. "I just left Travis Keene. He refused to speak to me. He cracked the door just enough for me to see the fear in his eyes. He's ready to talk, but only to you."

My pulse kicks. "Did he ask for me by name?"

"He asked for the *lady detective*. You're the only one associated with this case who matches that description." She lets out a sharp exhale. "Travis keeps a sailboat at Patriots Landing Marina. The *Good Golly, Miss Molly*—Dock B, slip forty-three. He wants you to meet him there at nine o'clock tonight."

"And let me guess. He wants me to come alone?" I ask, already knowing the answer.

"Yep. He insisted, actually. I personally don't think that's a good idea. Maybe you should take Briggs with you."

Irritation clenches my jaw. "Why? Because he's a man?" I say flatly. "I'm a trained professional, Alex. You don't need to worry about me. Besides, Briggs is intentionally keeping his distance from the jurors."

"I hope you know what you're doing," she says in a skeptical tone.

I'm not at all sure what I'm doing. But since I'm currently flying solo, what choice do I have?

"I'll be fine. But Alex, if Travis is scared enough to request a secret meeting, we should stop the interviews for now. I don't want to put anyone else in danger."

I end the call, stare at the slip number on my notepad, and feel the first cold twist settle in my gut. Nine o'clock can't come soon enough.

Chapter Eleven

I haven't been back to Patriots Landing since Ben's arrest. As I walk past his houseboat, a shadow moves behind the blinds—unmistakably his silhouette. My chest tightens at the sight of him. He's been through hell these past two months. Losing Addie, the love of his life, and their unborn child. Being framed for her murder. Nearly dying when the Old Guard tried to suicide him. And now Clay's acquittal—on top of everything else.

I slow, a heaviness settling in my chest. Is Ben still in danger? If Addie confided anything about her husband's extracurricular activities—the egg trafficking and Lord knows what else—the Old Guard might see him as unfinished business.

I make a mental note to check on him soon and continue down Dock B to slip forty-three. The *Good Golly, Miss Molly* is a majestic beauty—around fifty feet long with a sleek white hull and polished teak trim. A blue canvas Bimini shades the cockpit, flapping gently in the evening breeze.

I step aboard and knock lightly on the cabin door. It cracks open, and a pair of hazel eyes peer out at me. Bourbon fumes hit me before he even speaks.

"Show me your credentials," he demands.

I flash him the badge Morales gave me.

His gaze darts right, then left, then back to me. "Were you followed?"

"No. I made certain I wasn't." I don't tell him it took three detours and one sudden U-turn to lose Shadow Man on my way here.

He steps aside, letting me in, then closes and locks the door behind us.

The man standing in front of me has aged ten years since the verdict. His brown hair is streaked with new gray, and his eyes are sunken, rimmed with dark circles.

He gestures at an empty chair and drops onto the small, threadbare sofa. An open bottle of Maker's Mark sits on the table. He pushes it toward me. "Want some? It's all I have to offer."

I hold up my hand. "I'm fine, thanks."

"Suit yourself," he mutters, taking a swig straight from the bottle.

I lean forward. "Talk to me, Travis. I'm here to help."

He shakes his head, shoulders trembling. "Everyone else has betrayed me. How do I know I can trust you?" A loud sob rips out of him, and he buries his face in the crook of his arm.

I should record this—every word could be evidence. But Travis is barely holding it together, drunk and terrified. One wrong move, and he'll clam up completely. I commit every detail to memory instead.

I give him a moment until his breathing evens out. "Addie Dalton was my best friend," I say softly. "I'm seeking justice for her senseless death."

Travis drags his arm away from his face and rubs his eyes with both fists. "I thought they'd leave me alone after the trial."

My pulse ticks up. "Who is *they*?"

"Two of the jurors, Tommy Griggs and Gina Crenshaw. They're the puppets. I'm not sure who was pulling their strings."

The hair on the back of my neck prickles. "Okay. Let's start at the beginning."

He nods, grabs the Maker's bottle again, and sinks back into the sofa cushions. "Tommy and Gina were conducting secret meetings after hours—during the trial. They even came to see me."

I frown. "Discussing the case outside of deliberations is a violation of the court's instructions."

"I'm aware. But they didn't seem to care."

"What were these meetings about?" I ask, though I already suspect the answer.

"They were pressuring the undecided jurors to vote not guilty. Gina especially. She was like a rabid pit bull, determined to get Clay off no matter the cost."

"Were there undecided jurors besides you?"

He shakes his head, eyes unfocused. "It's hard to know for sure. In the beginning, Debbie Holleran and Patty Jo Sykes appeared to have an open mind about the case. But then, their attitudes just changed." He snaps his fingers. "Out of the blue, they were suddenly certain Clay was innocent."

"Are you sure Tommy and Gina persuaded them to change their minds?"

"I can't prove anything. I'm just telling you what I observed. Something happened. I could see it in their faces." Travis's head drops to his chest, and I think he's crying again.

I wait for him to compose himself before asking, "When did they come to see you?"

"Wednesday night." He swallows hard. "We got into a heated argument, and I threatened to call the police. They finally left. The next morning, I told Renee Mullins—our foreperson—that she needed to talk to the judge. But she refused. So I reported it myself, straight to Judge Tate. And he . . ." Travis lets out a broken laugh. "He basically called me a liar."

My stomach knots. "What happened after that?"

He wipes his nose with the back of his hand. "I got a phone call that night. The caller used some kind of voice distortion—mechanical, creepy as hell—and said my daughter would grow up without a father if I didn't vote not guilty." His voice trembles.

"They left me no choice. I had to protect my family. But my conscience wouldn't let me acquit a man I was sure was guilty. So I made up an excuse. My wife's mother is in a nursing home in Richmond. I told the judge she'd taken a turn for the worse. We packed up and left town before sunrise Friday."

"So what's got you running so scared now?"

"They're still after me," he whispers. "Because I didn't play their game. And because they know I can blow the whole thing wide open if I talk." His hand shakes as he rubs his jaw. "They're threatening me. Calling at all hours. Following me. This morning, I found this under my windshield." He removes a crumpled, folded paper from his pocket and hands it to me.

Scrawled in messy handwriting and smeared with ink is a short message.

Talk, and you're a dead man.

Taped to the bottom is a nine-millimeter bullet.

I wave the paper at him. "Did you report this to the authorities?"

He barks out a humorless laugh. "That's why you're here. I don't trust the rest of the deputies in the sheriff's department. Can you believe Boone put Clay back on staff? How screwed up is that?"

I shake my head. "Pretty screwed up. But, Travis, I'm no longer with the local sheriff's department."

I pat my pocket where the badge rests. "This is a Richmond PD credential. I'm consulting on a case tied to Addie's murder—a case that could bring down the Old Guard. But it's still in the early stages."

He stares at me, confused. "So you can't help me?"

I take a slow breath. "I can help you tell the truth—when the time comes."

His face crumples. "Then I'm a dead man. No one will believe me. I have no evidence—except that." He jabs a shaky finger at the note. "And they'll say I faked it."

"Things in Tidewell are volatile right now. I can't offer you the kind of protection you need here. Can you go back to Richmond for a while? A couple of weeks, maybe?"

He slumps back. "Not Richmond. Somewhere else. I have a plan." His eyes flick nervously toward the window. "I can't say more. I have a feeling they're listening."

"Probably." I stand abruptly. "Come on, Travis. Let me drive you home."

"No!" His hand shoots out, bourbon sloshing from the bottle. "I'm staying here tonight."

"That's not a good idea, Travis."

"I'm better off here . . . on the boat . . . not at home." His words slur, thick with bourbon. "They won't go near my wife and little girl. They want me, not them."

Something cold slides down my spine. "Your family shouldn't be alone."

"They're safer without me." His eyes drift toward me, haunted, cornered, begging for a way out. "If I go home, I lead them right to the door. But if I'm here . . . " He gestures weakly around the cabin. "They can only get me."

I kneel beside him. "Travis, listen to me. You don't have to face this alone."

He gives me a sad, lopsided smile. "I understand you can't protect me. And it's okay. Really."

It's not okay. Not even close. But he's too drunk to move and too terrified to think straight. And I can't drag a grown man off his own boat.

I pick up his phone from the coffee table and enter my contact information. "You have my number. Lock the door after I leave, and call me if anything feels off."

He nods—the kind of nod people give when they've already surrendered to something dark.

As I step back onto the dock, I can't shake the feeling I'm

walking away from a man who won't see morning.

Back inside my Bronco, doors locked, I take a steadying breath and call Briggs.

He picks up on the second ring. "Lane! I was about to call you. Did you see Alex's interview with Gina Crenshaw just now?"

My stomach drops. "No. What happened?"

Briggs lets out a short, incredulous breath. "Gina came after her with a baseball bat—chased Alex clean off her property."

"Gina is scared, which means Alex is over the target. I just left Travis Keene. He's sitting on testimony that could prove jury tampering. The problem is, they've put a target on his back. He's being threatened and followed—the whole nine yards. Any thoughts on how we protect him?"

Briggs exhales hard. "Unfortunately, I have no resources as long as Boone's running the sheriff's office."

"That's what I figured, but I had to ask." I glance in the rearview at Shadow Man, who's hugging my bumper as usual. "This is heating up, Briggs. I warned Alex to back off the juror interviews. She wouldn't listen to me. Maybe she'll listen to you," I say, ending the call.

I barrel down the road with Shadow Man glued to my tail, Briggs's words echoing in the Bronco. *I have no resources as long as Boone's running the sheriff's office.*

I consider my other options—Morales, protective custody, state police. Any kind of formal protection would mean paperwork, witnesses, jurisdiction—time I don't have. Time *Travis Keene* doesn't have.

I'm passing the entrance to Founders Park when Shadow Man suddenly drops back and a large vehicle—a jacked-up truck with blue lights flashing on the dash—whips in behind me.

I check my speedometer. Five miles over. No cop I know wastes ink on anything under ten.

I slow and pull to the shoulder. The black pickup noses in behind. The vanity plates read *OUTLAW.*

In my side mirror, I watch Colter Craddock climb out of the

driver's side and strut toward me. *Outlaw? Who does this punk think he is?*

I roll down my window. "You'd better have a badge to go with those blue lights."

He flashes it, smug as hell.

I tilt my head, unimpressed. "Boone must be desperate."

"With the curfew in place, the department is busier than usual." He braces an arm on the roof of my Bronco and leans in, invading my space. "And speaking of curfew, looks like you're breaking it again."

"I'm working."

His brow lifts. "Working? Last I heard, Boone canned you. I need proof of employment."

Anger flares as I flash my badge. "You're taking this Big Brother thing too far. And for the record, Boone did not can me. I quit."

He studies the badge. "Richmond PD? You're out of your jurisdiction."

"I'm consulting on a case with Sergeant Joe Morales. A *real crime* case. Call him. He'll vouch for me."

His eyes linger on my face a beat too long.

"Whatever game you think you're playing," I say coolly, "you might want to rethink it. I'm not here by accident."

He reaches in and brushes a strand of hair off my cheek. "I like spunky women. What say you and I have ourselves a little rendezvous later?"

I smack his hand away. "Touch me again, and I'm filing a complaint."

He straightens, smile gone. "Don't bother. You're too old for me anyway."

He pulls out his ticket pad and starts writing.

"Why are you writing me up? I just told you I'm working."

He purses his lips. "Sorry. Unless you can provide documentation for this *real crime* case you're supposedly working on, I have to write you up."

I let out a loud huff. "Whatever. I'll pay the fine. Just write the ticket."

"There's no fine for repeat offenders," he says, enjoying himself far too much. "You'll have to appear before Judge Tate in magistrate's court."

That does it.

"I'm done with this conversation," I snap, throwing the Bronco into gear.

Gravel spits as I pull away. In the mirror, Colter stands there, ticket pad in hand, watching me go. He shrugs. This wasn't a traffic stop. It was a warning.

And I walked right into his trap. I gave too much away. *I'm not here by accident.* I never should've mentioned Morales. If Colter runs his mouth to the wrong people, they'll know I'm asking questions I shouldn't be.

Chapter Twelve

I'm drinking coffee with Dad on Wednesday morning, the television tuned to local Richmond news, when a breaking story interrupts the extended weather forecast.

Footage of a burning building appears.

"Where is that?" I lower my cup. "Do I know that building?"

The camera pans to an attractive reporter, bundled up against the cold in a cherry-red parka, scarf, and knit cap. "We're coming to you live from Willow Creek Fertility Clinic, where a fire is currently burning out of control. Fire crews have been on scene for approximately fifteen minutes and are working to contain a blaze that appears confined to the cryogenic laboratory—the separate building that houses the clinic's storage tanks."

The reporter glances behind her as another burst of flames shoots up from the roof.

"While the cause of the fire is still unknown, we've been told that this clinic houses multiple cryogenic storage units containing harvested eggs and fertilized embryos. At this time, we do not have confirmation on whether those units are in danger or if they've been successfully protected."

Another boom from inside the building startles the reporter.

"We'll continue to monitor the situation and bring you updates as soon as we learn more."

A slow, sick certainty settles in my gut.

I replay my exchange with Colter from last night. *Is it possible—*

Before I can finish my thought, my phone lights up with Morales's name. I snatch it off the counter. "Morning."

"Can you talk?" His tone tells me he won't take *no* for an answer.

I glance at Dad, who's watching me with that raised-brow, *I know something's up* look. "Give me a minute."

I press the phone to my chest. "I need to take this, Dad. I'm going outside. You wait here for Lally. She'll be here any minute."

Sliding off the stool, I grab my coat, call for Scout, and step outside to the patio, where frosted air bites my face.

"I was just watching the news about the fire," I tell Morales. "I was worried something like this might happen. If there was any evidence left in that clinic, it just went up in flames."

"Yep." Paper rustles on his end. "I've been digging on my side. The reports of the break-in at Ellison's office are gone. Vanished. And we're getting more and more calls from Ellison's patients about their missing eggs."

"Who's been responding to these calls?" I ask.

"I assume Milo has," Morales says flatly. "But no reports have been filed."

"You *assume*? Have you questioned Milo about it?"

He lets out a loud sigh. "Not yet, Lane. You can trust that I'm looking into it. I will defend Milo until I have reason not to. Just as I would defend you."

I'm not so sure about that, but I hold my tongue.

"Yes, sir. I hear you loud and clear." I chew on a hangnail, debating whether to bring up last night's incident. "There's something else I should mention. I had an exchange with Colter Craddock last night, and I may have let slip that I'm consulting with

Richmond on a case. Specifically, that I'm working with you. I doubt he will, but he may call for confirmation."

"Thanks for the heads up. I haven't heard the Craddock name in a long time. Any relation to Colt Craddock?"

I blink hard. "Geez, Sarge. Do you know everyone in this state?"

Morales chuckles. "Feels like it sometimes. How old is Colter?"

"Early twenties. Big boy with an even larger attitude."

"That would make the Colt Craddock I knew his grandfather. He was the sleaziest, slimiest politician ever to hold office in Virginia. He represented the Northern Neck in some capacity or other. I can't remember now. He made a run for governor once. Fortunately, my fellow Virginians had enough sense not to elect him." He pauses a beat. "He was a legend, Lane. Not the good kind. What sort of exchange did you have with his grandson?"

The memory of Colter brushing a strand of hair off my face makes me shiver.

"Remember? I told you about the Night Ryders. Boone has now deputized them to enforce the curfew. I was out after dark, and Colter pulled me over. He's trying to ruffle my feathers. Nothing I can't handle. Yet."

"Be careful. Sounds like they are not messing around." He pauses. "So how much did you tell him?"

"Just what I said. That I'm consulting with you on a real crime case. What if that got back to Milo? What if they suspect I'm investigating them? What if he passed it on to the egg traffickers?"

A long silence. When he speaks again, his voice is low. "You need proof, Lane. You can't assume that either Milo or the Old Guard is involved in this operation."

I roll my eyes. Of course he's protecting Milo. "That's fair about Milo. But Addie's spreadsheets point to the Old Guard. What if they found out about my encounter with Colter?"

"Whoever started that fire was covering their tracks. Maybe you spooked them. Or maybe the people running this operation were already one step ahead. Either way, the fire was going to happen eventually."

"You're probably right," I say reluctantly. "So what do we do now?"

"We move carefully," Morales says. "Keep your eyes open and document everything. I'll do the same here. This situation is too hot. It's going to explode sooner or later."

"Got it." I end the call and stuff the phone into my coat pocket. Gazing back at the house, I spot movement in the windows. Nine o'clock has come and gone. Lally is now at the stove, making Dad breakfast, and Shawna's perched in her usual chair.

I want more coffee, but I don't dare disrupt their balance—an old man and his caregivers moving through a fragile morning routine. It's hard to believe his brilliant career on the circuit court bench has been reduced to this.

I drop some logs into the fire pit, the kindling flaring at the touch of a match. Morales is right. Whether or not my exchange with Colter sped things up, Willow Creek was already a target. It was only a matter of time before someone burned it down.

I hold my hands close to the fire, warming them, while I look out over the water. Despite the crisp air, it's a beautiful morning—clear blue sky, sun dancing off the creek like diamonds. A bald eagle glides overhead, wings spread wide, and settles in the top of a nearby pine.

I long to be in Richmond, where the action is. But showing up now would tip off the Old Guard for sure. And once they feel pressure, someone's liable to get hurt. Dad's in the house, and the eagle's overhead. I'm where I need to be. For now.

My phone vibrates in my pocket with an incoming text, a photo from Amanda—Milo in profile, the clinic burning behind him, a self-satisfied smirk on his face.

Another buzz signals a string of texts from Amanda.

He's actually enjoying this.

Maybe he lit the match himself.

Something's up with him.

Hushed phone calls. Unexplained disappearances.

He's neck-deep in whatever this is.

I fire off my response.

Thanks! Keep an eye on him and send anything else you see.

Lally emerges through the French doors with a coffee mug in one hand and my knit cap, gloves, and scarf in the other.

She shivers. "Brr. It's freezing. What're you doing out here?"

I flash her my phone. "Networking."

"Well, you need to bundle up." Handing me the coffee, she tugs the wool cap over my head and drapes the scarf around my neck like she did when I was a child.

I smile softly at her. "Thank you, Lally. I could get used to you pampering me."

She beams. "That's the idea. I got some biscuits in the oven. I'll bring you one when they come out."

My stomach growls at the thought of a warm, buttery biscuit smothered in honey. "Yum. Bring two, please."

She laughs. "You got it."

I wait until she goes back inside before calling Chloe. The blare of sirens in the background tells me she's at the scene. "Morning, Chloe. I've been watching the news coverage of the fire. I'm so sorry."

"I can't hear you—hang on." A rustling sound is followed by the slamming of a car door. The audio clicks over to Bluetooth. "Sorry. It's so loud out there I can't think straight." She lets out an audible sigh. "This is bad, Lane."

"The news reporter said the fire was contained to the cryogenic lab. Is that true?"

"Yes! They were able to save the clinic, thank goodness. But the lab equipment—the tanks, the freezers—all of that is gone." Chloe's voice wavers. "I'm so done with Dr. Ellison and that clinic. I've already contacted my recruiter. I'm officially looking for a new job. Maybe I'll move near you. What's the name of your town again?"

"Tidewell. But trust me, you don't want to live here. Not right now. We've got our own problems. But Richmond has plenty of opportunities for experienced nurses."

"You're right. I'm not worried. I'll find something." Her voice cracks. "I just feel so awful for our patients. Some of them have been trying for years, and now . . . their eggs, their embryos . . . It's all gone."

"Is there no chance of saving them?" I ask quietly.

"None. The cryo tanks are built to hold liquid nitrogen at minus 196 Celsius, but they're not fireproof. If the heat gets too high, the tanks will fail. Once they warm even a little, the eggs start to thaw. And once they thaw . . ." She swallows hard. "There's no reversing it. The fire chief says the building is threatening to collapse. The roof could go any minute."

"Do they know how the fire started?"

"They suspect arson. One of the firemen mentioned gasoline. I'm not surprised—are you?"

"Not after everything that's happened."

She exhales a shaky breath. "There's this one patient . . . saddest story ever. Her husband died two months ago, and she was scheduled to have their fertilized embryo implanted this morning."

My chest tightens. "Oh, Chloe, that's awful."

"I know, right? I can't stop thinking about her." Chloe's voice quivers as though she's near tears.

"Keep me posted. And stay in touch, okay?"

"I will," she says, and the line goes dead.

My throat tightens. With grief. But also anger.

Embryos, eggs—women's last chances of having children—left

to burn because despicable men saw profit where there should have been protection, and treated women's bodies like merchandise.

Whoever did this didn't just destroy evidence. They destroyed lives.

Chapter Thirteen

I pace the patio, toss more logs on the fire, throw the ball for Scout—anything to push the image of the burning cryogenic lab out of my mind. When nothing works, I stop fighting my conscience.

Where's the harm in driving to Richmond? I'll stay out of sight, keep to the periphery. But I need to be there—to feel the pulse of it, to see the scene with my own eyes.

Scout trots at my heels as I gather my things and grab two biscuits from Lally on the way out. Scout hasn't ridden shotgun with me in weeks, and I'm grateful for the company. I tune into a Richmond news station as we pull onto the road, listening to commentators speculate about arson being the cause of the Willow Creek fire. About why anyone would want to torch a lab housing human eggs.

If only they knew.

I'm crossing over the bridge out of Tidewell when Briggs calls.

"Where are you?" he snaps.

"On my way to Richmond. The Willow Creek cryo lab caught fire last night."

"I heard." His voice dips. "You might want to detour by

Patriots Landing. Travis Keene has disappeared. The sheriff has declared him officially missing."

I palm the steering wheel. "Damn it! I knew I shouldn't have left him last night."

"He's missing, Lane. That doesn't mean he's dead."

"True. He mentioned having an escape plan. With any luck, he's far from Tidewell by now." I make a sharp U-turn back toward town. "I'm on my way."

"I'll meet you there," Briggs says, and the line goes dead.

Squad cars choke the parking lot at the marina. I pull into the first open spot and let Scout out. She bolts straight toward Ben's dock—muscle memory guiding her steps. She hasn't forgotten the time she spent here with Addie.

I hurry after her, and when Ben's houseboat comes into view, she erupts into frantic barking. A disheveled Ben steps onto the stern, squinting against the sun. His dark hair is a mess, his eyes bloodshot—he looks like he hasn't slept since the verdict.

"What's going on?" he calls, lifting a hand to block the glare. Then he spots Scout, and something in him softens. She launches herself aboard, and he drops to his knees, letting her drown him in licks.

A hoarse laugh breaks from him. "I've missed you too, girl."

Seeing him like this—the man who loved Addie most—makes my chest tighten. Addie, Ben, and Scout were a little trio. If life had taken a kinder turn, Ben and Addie would've married and raised their baby together, maybe even right here on this houseboat—their love shack on the water.

I don't condone extramarital affairs. My husband's infidelity tore my own marriage apart. But Addie and Ben were different. They were high school sweethearts—each other's firsts. Addie broke things off to attend cosmetology school. Years later, she married Clay. When the marriage began to unravel, she turned to Ben for help. One thing led to another, and they fell back in love.

Some loves don't disappear. They just wait.

Ben tosses his chin at the cluster of deputies at the end of the dock. "What's going on?"

"Travis Keene went missing."

A shadow crosses his face, the kind that comes from seeing too much. He nods once, slow, unsurprised. "When?"

"Sometime last night. Maybe early this morning. I'm not sure yet." I study him. "Have you seen anything unusual in the past twenty-four hours?"

He huffs a humorless breath. "I see everything around here, Lane. Most of it's unusual." His dark, hollow eyes lock on mine, and something inside me buckles. *Does he know I was here last night?*

I force an awkward laugh. "Fair enough."

Ben rises, still scratching Scout behind the ears. "Dogs are a lot of responsibility, Lane. If you ever have to go out of town—or just need a break—I'd be happy to keep her for you."

I glance over at Scout, who's pressing herself against Ben's leg. "I'm sure she'd love to have some Ben time. We'll make it happen soon."

"Good. I'm pretty much always available."

My heart pinches at the sadness under his words. He's a commercial fisherman. On a cold, bright morning like this, he should be out on the water. Did he call in sick? Is he even working at all anymore? I don't ask.

"Come on, girl." I slap my leg, and she hops off the boat.

"If you think of anything that might help locate Travis," I add, "let the authorities know."

"I'd rather swallow poison than talk to them," he mutters. "You still working with Boone?"

I hesitate—just long enough for the silence to say more than I intend.

"No," I say finally. "One month was enough. I'm doing a little investigating of my own."

Before he can press for details, I turn and head up the dock, Scout trotting at my side.

As I approach Travis's boat, I groan under my breath. Colter Craddock is standing with the others, hands on his hips, like a legitimate law enforcement officer—not an imposter. What the hell is Boone thinking, deputizing someone with no training?

I wedge myself into the group beside Briggs. "Where are we?" I whisper.

"Travis's wife reported him missing late last night." Briggs jerks a thumb toward the parking lot. "His truck's still here. His phone's dead. Crime unit's onboard. So far they've only turned up an empty bottle of Maker's Mark."

Colter steps forward, waving a black-and-white photograph of me leaving Travis's boat last night. "And this. Appears you were the last one to see him," he says, smug as a cat with feathers in its teeth.

I keep my face neutral, even as my heart slams against my ribs. *So that's how they're going to play it.* Travis didn't act on his escape plan. They killed him, and now they're setting me up to take the fall. Two birds. One stone.

"Maybe I was. Maybe I wasn't," I say coolly. "When I left here around nine thirty, he was still alive. Maybe a little drunk. Okay— a lot drunk. You've got surveillance photos, which means you had eyes on his boat. So tell me—how did you lose him?"

Colter opens his mouth to speak, but no words come out.

"What's wrong, Colter? Cat got your tongue?" I pin Boone with a stare sharp enough to cut glass. "This is what happens when you deputize rookies."

"Watch it, Lane," Briggs mutters from the side of his mouth.

"I'm just getting started, actually." I fold my arms. "Colter, remind me again—how many minutes after you pulled me over last night did Travis disappear? Maybe if you'd been solving real crimes instead of playing traffic cop to hit on women, Travis might still be alive."

A few deputies shift, uncomfortable. *Touch a nerve.*

My gaze sweeps the circle. "So . . . here's my question for you, gentlemen. Who assigned Colter to a missing-persons investigation involving a juror with documented threats against him? Anyone want to take credit?"

No one speaks.

I lock eyes with the sheriff. "Boone? Did you—or is this Clay's handiwork? Acquitted or not, half this town still sleeps with their doors locked because of him. And now he's calling shots in the sheriff's office? That's one hell of a promotion."

Boone's face goes so red he looks like he might stroke out. "You're a loose cannon, Sutherlin," he growls.

"Oh, I'm a cannon all right," I fire back. "And you loaded it. You want to talk about what you did to me nineteen years ago, Boone? Because I can assure you—I haven't forgotten."

A heavy silence drops over the dock. Even I feel the line I've crossed.

"That's enough." Briggs clamps a hand around my arm and steers me away fast. Scout whimpers and trots after us.

Briggs hauls me halfway down the dock before he stops short and whirls on me. "Are you outta your mind? You just wrote your own death warrant. You pissed off every law enforcement officer in this county."

I yank my arm free. "Good."

He blinks at me. "Good?"

"Yes, good." My breath comes hard, hot in the cold air. "I'd bet my life that Travis's body is at the bottom of Oyster Bay. When it surfaces, they're going to pin his murder on me."

Briggs swears under his breath and scrubs a hand over his face. "You don't know that."

"The hell I don't," I snap. "They've got surveillance of me leaving his boat. I was the last person to see him alive. Colter pulled me over on my way home—timed to the minute. They're building the case already."

He grips my shoulders, forcing me to meet his eyes. "Lane. Stop. You can't go around throwing matches in a fireworks factory because you're scared."

"I'm not scared," I say, voice steel.

"Liar! You're terrified." His tone softens but stays tight. "And with good reason. But you can't go to war with the whole sheriff's office."

I swallow. Hard. "I just did. Because I don't have a choice. If I don't start swinging, they're going to bury me alive."

Briggs's jaw flexes. "What was that nineteen-years-ago business? Boone looked ready to keel over. What did he do to you?"

"I don't want to talk about it." I step back, Scout glued to my leg. "The important thing is, Boone knows exactly what I meant."

The adrenaline fades, and reality hits hard.

I acted carelessly—same reckless behavior Morales benched me for. And this time, I won't be the only one who pays.

I'm living at River Birch now with Dad, Judd, Brandy, and their unborn child.

And I just brought the storm straight to our doorstep.

Chapter Fourteen

I abandon my mission to Richmond. I'm in no shape to make the trip now. While I'd rather drive straight to River Birch, crawl under a rock, and pretend the rest of the world doesn't exist, Briggs insists we go for coffee to plan my next move.

And he's right. I need to decompress, assess the damage, lick the battle wounds.

On the way to Salty Bean, it hits me like a gut punch. Briggs distanced himself from me in order to save face with Tate. But he very publicly saved my butt at the marina, and now I've dragged him into the storm too.

Every deputy on the dock saw him pull me away. The line has clearly been drawn—them versus me—and Briggs is now standing on my side. The wrong side. Boone will bury him. Tate will fire him. And if the Old Guard decides he's a problem, they may do even worse.

Briggs gains nothing from partnering with me. The problem is, he won't listen if I tell him to walk away. He'll either pull the big-brother routine, act like he's obligated to protect me, or he'll claim he has skin in the game. I need to put an end to this. At least for now. He may not see it this way, but I'm doing him a favor. Maybe even saving his life. One day, he'll thank me.

I've never been a team player anyway. From now on, I'm flying solo.

The opportunity for a public scene practically hands itself to me when we're stuck in the long line at Salty Bean.

"Is that Alex ahead of us?" I ask, rising on my toes to look past the cluster of people.

"Probably. I told her to meet us here."

I stiffen. "Why would you do that without asking me? I'm not in the mood for her today." I step out of line, slinging my bag over my shoulder. "I'm leaving."

Briggs catches my arm. "Why are you so threatened by her?"

The question lands harder than I expect. And now, I'm legitimately irked. "What makes you think I'm threatened by her?"

"It's obvious." His voice is maddeningly calm. "Is it her looks? Her success?"

Irritation crawls under my skin like fire ants. "You're out of line."

He tilts his head, studying me. "You know, you're pretty too?"

I roll my eyes. "Great. Runner-up. Just what every girl wants."

"You're being ridiculous," he says, exhaling. "Honestly? I think all women intimidate you."

The truth hurts—especially when it hits dead center. I've always been more comfortable with men. My so-called girl squad is thin. Thinner now that Addie's gone. I have people I can call in a crisis. I just don't have women who linger.

Briggs follows me outside, and the argument detonates—real this time, not staged.

He unloads, hurling insults—some justified, some not.

Scout growls at his feet, but he doesn't stop.

Reckless. Obsessive. A danger to myself and everyone around me.

I swallow past the lump in my throat. "Don't hold back, Briggs. Tell me how you really feel."

He scrubs his hands through his hair. "What you did this morning was stupid, Lane."

"There it is." My voice rises. "What would you have done—let them arrest me? They're trying to take me down. I'm not going quietly."

"You'll go down all right. All the way to the bottom of Oyster Bay with Travis Keene."

The words hit like a body blow. Tears press hot behind my eyes, but I refuse to let him see me break. "Goodbye, Briggs."

I spin on my heel. He hurries after me.

"Lane—wait." His voice cracks. "I shouldn't have said that. I'm worried about you. About your family. About me."

I turn to face him, walking backward. "Snip snip." I mime scissors. "Cord severed. You're free of me."

He lowers his voice. "I don't want to be free of you. But I also don't want to lose my job. If we're going to save this town, we need the power behind my office."

"Not *we*, Briggs. Not anymore. From here on out, I go it alone." I shoo him away. "Go back to your girlfriend. Team up with her. I'm sure she's not reckless. Or obsessive. Or a danger to everyone around her."

I reach my Bronco, open the door for Scout, and she leaps into the backseat. I slam the door and peel off down Main Street in the direction opposite home.

I drive like a maniac, taking sharp corners, cutting through alleys, and doubling back until I'm sure Shadow Man is lost in the fumes behind me.

I don't slow down until I reach our tree-lined driveway.

Inside the house, I lock every door, check them twice, then retreat to the basement workroom. The air is cool and still. The faint smell of gun oil calms my mind.

I line up Dad's guns on the workbench—shotgun, revolver, and the semi-automatic rifle I gave him for Christmas years ago. I'm not sure he's ever even fired it.

I clean each weapon slowly. Methodical. Mechanical. Preparing for whatever or whoever comes next. Fear hums under my skin—the old kind, the kind I thought I'd buried nineteen years ago. And deep in my bones, I know the storm I brought to our doorstep is closing in.

With Briggs out of my life, I can better focus on the mission. *Missions.*

Time is running thin. When Travis's body floats to the surface —tomorrow, next week, whenever the current gives him back— Boone and Clay will move fast. They'll spin a story before I can blink.

Lane Sutherlin. Unhinged vigilante, former detective. Violent. Obsessed. The last person to see him alive. Motive TBD. Judge Tate will rush the case to trial. And this time, the tampered jury will convict.

I oil the rifle barrel with steady hands, but my mind is anything but.

The egg trafficking is my only way through. But I need evidence. Hard evidence—not Addie's spreadsheets, not Chloe's hunches. Something that can survive Boone, Tate, and the shadow army they've built.

A knot twists my gut. There's more to the fire at the lab than meets the eye.

What am I missing? Insurance fraud? Those tanks are worth hundreds of thousands—maybe more. That would point to an inside job. One of Ellison's partners. A desperate investor. Someone cornered.

But the timing is too perfect. Too surgical. This wasn't panic.

Maybe it wasn't just cleanup. Maybe it was a message. Or something deeper—something with roots I still can't see.

If they wiped Ellison's databases, silenced her, covered their tracks—why burn the lab at all?

Unless . . .

A theory slams into me, breath-stealing and ugly. Every missing piece and impossible coincidence slams together with a force that sends me rocketing off the stool. My pulse hammers as I pace around the basement, the truth igniting all at once.

But until I can back it up, it's nothing more than a nightmare masquerading as logic.

I pick up my phone and fire off a text to Morales.

> Has anyone pulled exterior surveillance from the cryo lab?

His reply comes fast.

> I'm one step ahead of you. Cameras went down two days before the fire. Footage wiped.

I respond.

> Interesting timing. Did you ask Milo about them?

> Yep. He got a little squirrelly. But I'm not jumping the gun. The jury's still out on him.

Of course it is.

A cold weight settles in my stomach. It explains everything. Everything except how the heck I'm supposed to prove it alone.

Chapter Fifteen

A shift in the house—a creak in the floorboard, a rush of cold air—jerks me awake seconds before the sleigh bells on the rolling wardrobe at the front door jangle violently. The click of the lock—then the security alarm blasts through the silence.

I bolt out of bed, sprinting down the stairs barefoot, heart punching against my ribs. Scout barrels after me, hackles up, whining low in her throat.

By the time I reach the center hallway, the front door is cracked open, frigid air knifing into the house.

Dad is already gone. I scan the hallway—his coat is still hanging on the rack.

For a panicked beat, I consider sending Scout after him, but if she loses the trail or runs into danger, they will both be gone.

Think, Lane. You won't get far half dressed in freezing temperatures.

Pivoting, I tear back up the stairs, two at a time. In my room, I throw on my clothes from yesterday and drop to my knees, yanking my *go bag* from under the bed—the one packed for nights like this. Binoculars. Burner phone. Pepper spray. Backup gun. My contingency plan for exactly the kind of nightmare unfolding right now.

I jam on my shoes, sling the bag over my shoulder, and whisper a prayer that Dad hasn't wandered far.

Hold on, Dad. I'm coming.

I slip outside with Scout on a leash beside me, the cold hitting us like a slap. It's barely five thirty, the world caught somewhere between night and dawn. Frost sheets the yard—sparkling silver over the grass, copper leaves underneath. The footprints—flat and smooth, the soft outline of his leather slippers—give Dad away instantly.

Scout noses one of the prints, whining softly, then lifts her head toward the woods.

"Yes," I whisper. "Go."

We follow the trail across the front lawn and pause at the edge of the woods, Scout straining against the leash.

For a split second, I debate taking the Bronco. A vehicle would be faster. Warmer. And if Dad wandered farther than I think, I could cover more ground.

But the crushed-frost footprints lead straight into the trees, sharp as breadcrumbs. If I take the Bronco, I'll lose his trail.

"On foot it is," I murmur.

I tighten my grip on Scout's leash and step beneath the tree canopy, where the frost thins but still clings to fallen leaves. These woods were my entire world once. Judd and Tommy and I spent entire summers here—building forts, playing war. I was always the nurse. I know every bend. Every old oak. Every place a person could hide.

But this morning, the woods feel different. Still. Spooky. The trees holding their collective breath.

I draw Scout a little closer as we follow Dad's footprints along the narrow path connecting River Birch to Founders Park.

"Dad," I murmur to the shadows, "where are you?"

When we reach the fork in the path, his prints veer right toward the old boathouse. The Tide House. Where I discovered Addie's body. Where Dad, who just happened to be fishing here at the time, was arrested for her murder. Of all places for him to wander . . . why there?

At the end of the path, when we emerge from the trees, I'm blinded by the glare of headlights. I step back into the woods. Peeking out from behind a large oak tree, I spot three vehicles—two pickups and a Tahoe—parked haphazardly at the entrance to the boathouse.

I ease the binoculars out of my bag and lift them to my eyes. Milo is huddled with Colt and Colter Craddock. Fear skates down my spine. What is Milo doing with them—meeting in the dark, at the crack of dawn, in Tidewell? It confirms what I've feared all along. Milo isn't an innocent bystander in this—he's in deep.

I crouch lower, slipping my phone from my pocket. Even at this distance, the zoom picks up enough detail to make out their silhouettes—Milo's hulking outline, Colt's narrow stance, Colter's restless pacing. I snap several photos in quick succession, angling for anything usable.

Grainy or not, they're time-stamped. Proof that the Craddock brothers and Milo McDermott were meeting in secret at dawn. Proof I'll need.

If only I could hear what they're saying . . .

I slip around to the water side of the Tide House, keeping low, Scout pressed against my leg. Through the rotted slats, their voices carry—Colter's deep drawl, Colt's nasal rasp, Milo's jittery mumble. They're close enough that every word vibrates through the damp boards.

" . . . She's getting too close," Colt says.

"Mark my words, she'll get closer if we don't stop her," Milo replies. "That bitch has been a thorn in my side from the beginning." He lets out a malicious bark of laughter I recognize instantly. "I get to do the honors."

My pulse stutters. Ice washes down my spine.

"No way, dude," Colter cuts in. "That's my job."

A loud bang comes from inside the boathouse. Scout freezes,

ears pinned flat. I clamp a hand over her muzzle, my breath locked tight in my chest.

Please don't let it be Dad.

"Hey, did you hear that?" Milo asks.

"Probably a raccoon," Colt says.

"No," Colter insists. "Sounded bigger."

"Let's check inside," Milo says. "Just in case."

My blood goes cold.

Their boots thud across the dock. The boathouse door slams open. I can't see inside. I can only hear their movements.

A beat of silence—

Then Colter's triumphant voice. "Well, lookee here."

"Son of a—who the hell is that?" Colt demands.

Milo's nervous laugh ricochets off the wooden walls. "Looks like a vagrant to me. Wandered in off the street, looking for a warm place to sleep."

Colt snorts. "In flannel pajamas and leather slippers? Drag him out."

A scuffle follows, and then a yelp—not loud but wounded and confused and undeniably Dad's.

I choke down a cry and press myself flatter against the siding.

"What're you doing here, Grandpa?" Colter taunts.

Dad mumbles something—garbled, frightened.

Colter laughs, cruel and sharp. "Idiot doesn't even know his own name."

A thud—too heavy to be anything but Dad hitting the wall or floor.

Scout trembles violently. I hold her tight. My heart screams *Go to him.* My brain knows if I step in, they'll kill him. They'll kill us both.

"What do we do?" Colt asks. "He heard us talking. We can't just let him go."

"We could dump him," Milo offers. "Tide'll take him quick."

My whole body goes numb. I won't let that happen.

Dad whimpers—a small, broken sound that tears something deep inside me.

"Knock it off," Colt snaps. "Look at him."

A pause—long and assessing.

"He looks familiar to me," Colt finally says. "Do we know him?"

"I'm not sure. Maybe," Colter answers.

"Something's wrong with him," Colt says. "Man's half gone. He's got dementia or Alzheimer's. He won't remember a damn thing by lunch."

"I'm not so sure about that," Colter says.

"Then you do the job, son. I want no part of it," Colt says.

Milo exhales shakily. "Me either. I don't want the blood of some old, demented man on my hands."

Colter mutters, "I guess you're right. Looks like he's already been dead for years."

"Leave him," Colt says. "No one will believe a word he says. Let's go."

Boot steps shuffle. Someone spits. Then the door slams shut. Their voices fade. Their truck rumbles to life. They drive off.

Only then do I move. I rush to the front door—Scout darting ahead—and slip inside the dim, rotting boathouse.

My eyes adjust. And there he is. Dad. Crumpled on the floor, shoulders shaking, hands over his ears like he's trying to block out the world. A bruise already darkening along his jaw.

"Dad," I whisper, kneeling beside him.

He flinches like I'm one of them.

"It's me, Lane. You're safe, Dad. They're gone."

But he doesn't answer. Doesn't look at me. Just rocks, trembling, whispering something I can't make out.

I lean close.

"Don't . . ." His voice cracks. "Don't let them . . . bury the babies."

My heart stops. *Babies? What Babies?*

They broke him. And they will pay.

Chapter Sixteen

Two hours later, I'm stretched out on the sofa in the family room, phone pressed to my ear as the alarm company's tinny elevator music loops for the tenth time. Dad sits in the recliner beside me, nearly catatonic—hands slack, eyes unfocused, breathing shallow. He hasn't eaten. He hasn't spoken. He's barely even blinked since we got home from the Tide House.

When the mudroom door opens, I brace myself for my brother's wrath. If he told me to pack my bags and get out, I wouldn't argue. I failed at my job. I let Dad get out of the house in the middle of the night. The problem is, I have nowhere else to go.

"Morning," Judd calls out when he spots us.

I lift a hand in a half wave and point to the phone. "I'm on hold."

He passes through the breakfast room toward Dad. "Hey, Dad. How're you feeling today?"

No answer.

Judd kneels beside the recliner. "You okay?"

Silence. Not even a flicker of recognition.

He waves a hand in front of Dad's blank stare. "Hello. Anybody home?"

Still nothing.

Judd rises slowly, tension braced across his shoulders. "What's wrong with him, Lane? How long has he been like this?"

I swing my legs off the sofa. "Let's talk in the other room."

"Uh-oh. I don't like the sound of that," Judd says, following me into the kitchen.

While he pours himself a coffee, I tell him about Dad slipping out, the trail of footsteps through the woods, the boathouse, the Craddocks, Milo. I cast frequent glances toward the family room, to keep an eye on Dad, and because I can't bear to watch disappointment settle into my brother's face.

When I finally force myself to look at him, Judd doesn't seem angry. Or judgmental. He just looks . . . wrecked.

"What a bunch of bastards," he says, voice low and shaking with controlled fury. "How could they treat an old man like that? If I wasn't about to be a father, I'd kill the lot of them with my bare hands."

"Leave that to me," I say. "It's what I'm trained for."

Judd frowns, the lines in his forehead deepening. "If you followed him through the woods on foot, how'd you get him home? He's in no state to walk. Why didn't you call me?"

"I thought about it," I admit. "But I didn't want to bother you. I left Scout with him and ran home for the car."

He stares at me like I've lost my mind. "You *trusted* Scout to protect him? Give that dog a stale biscuit, and she'd sell us all out without blinking."

Despite everything, a small laugh escapes me. "She understood her job. She was sitting next to him, back straight and ears perked, when I got back."

"Only because no one offered her a snack." He shakes his head. "You got lucky this time, Lane. Really lucky. Things could've gone a lot worse for both you and Dad. We need to make sure this doesn't happen again."

I nod, pointing to the phone. "That's why I'm calling the alarm company. Our system is ancient. We need an upgrade—motion detectors at the stairs and in the hallway."

"Agreed. The sleigh bells aren't cutting it," he mutters.

I hold up a finger when a representative from the alarm company finally comes on the line. I explain the urgency of the situation—dementia, wandering, repeated break-outs—and she promises to send someone right away.

I end the call and turn to Judd. "Maybe we need to install a double-keyed deadbolt on the front door."

He raises his eyebrows. "What happens if the house catches on fire?"

"We can hide the key near the door?"

He lets out a dry laugh. "Brilliant idea. Dad can't remember his own name today, but he'll somehow remember to hunt for a secret key while flames lick at his flannel pajamas."

"Be serious, Judd. Someone will always be in the house with him. At least it will keep him from wandering. It's not foolproof, but it's the lesser evil."

Judd exhales, defeated. "Yeah. Okay. We'll do whatever keeps him alive. But talk to the technician first. He may have some better ideas."

My gaze drifts to Dad—still sitting in the recliner, staring through the wall like he's somewhere far away. "I'm worried about him. He's so out of it. Should I take him to the doctor?"

Judd rubs the back of his neck. "Let's give him some time. He went through hell this morning. Maybe once Lally gets here, he'll snap out of it."

A small weight lifts from my chest. "If anyone can get through to him, it's Lally."

But when Lally arrives thirty minutes later, Dad doesn't crack a joke or flirt with her like he usually does. He just stares at her, blank and distant, as though he can't place her. As though he doesn't know who she is.

His response to Shawna is even more unsettling. He normally takes a perverse pleasure in trying to get under her skin, but today, he doesn't acknowledge her at all.

I pull them aside and explain what happened at the boathouse. They agree to give him space, to let his system settle.

"Traumatic shocks can scramble a fragile mind," Shawna reminds us. "He just needs a little time."

Judd is shrugging into his jacket when the alarm technician pulls into the driveway. "I can stay if you need me," he offers, though the glance at his watch tells me he's pressed for time.

"You go on to work," I say. "I can handle this."

I greet the technician at the door and show him to the ancient control panel.

"Whoa," he whistles. "This thing came over on the Mayflower."

Under any other circumstances, I'd laugh.

The upgrade costs Dad a small fortune, but it buys me peace of mind. The technician installs motion sensors throughout the house and replaces the yellowed keypad with a modern, app-controlled panel. Then he adds smart keyless entry locks to every exterior door. They look unsightly against our old farmhouse architecture, which is why I didn't suggest them in the first place. But they're practical and safe, and for the first time all morning, I feel like we're taking a step—small but solid—toward protecting Dad from the world. And the world from Dad.

From the front doorway, I watch the technician's truck drive down the driveway. My pulse is still jumpy, my nerves still wired. Despite the new security system, every shadow in this house feels like a threat now. Every sound a warning.

I'm still standing in the doorway, my mind a million miles away, when the crunch of tires on gravel brings Scout to my side, the fur along her scruff bristling.

"Easy, girl," I murmur, unsure whether I'm trying to calm her or myself.

I expect to see the alarm technician barreling back down the driveway, having forgotten one of his tools. Instead, a sleek black Range Rover glides to a stop beside the old magnolia. My hand instinctively finds the Glock holstered at my hip. I don't know anyone who drives a Range Rover.

The engine cuts off, but no one gets out. The windows are tinted, preventing me from seeing inside.

I tighten my grip on my weapon. Is it the Craddocks? Did they figure out Dad was the one they roughed up in the boathouse? If so, why are they here? Surely, they didn't come to apologize. They must be covering their tracks. But in broad daylight?

The driver's door finally opens, and a woman steps out—mid-thirties with glossy chestnut hair pulled into a neat low twist. Her posture is impeccable. Her coat looks expensive. Not flashy—tasteful. A soft camel wool that probably costs more than my entire winter wardrobe.

And she's strikingly beautiful. Not intimidating—poised. Elegant. Like someone who could walk into any room and instantly raise the IQ level. Definitely *not* a Craddock.

She lifts a gloved hand to shade her eyes and scans the house, uncertainty crossing her face. When she spots me in the doorway, something in her expression—haunted, fragile—knocks the air right out of me. She's not here to hurt me. She's here because she needs something.

She approaches the porch slowly, hands clasped together, voice trembling just enough to betray the weight she's carrying. "Are you Detective Sutherlin?"

I straighten, swallowing whatever is left of the fear in my chest. "I am. Lane Sutherlin. Can I help you?"

Her eyes shine with unshed tears. "My name is Caroline Edwards. Chloe Morgan suggested I reach out to you, that you may be able to help me. She didn't have your address. Only that you live in Tidewell. The bartender at Slip99 . . . strange name . . . Cooter, I think . . . told me to try here."

I tilt my head. "Is this about the fire?"

She bites on her lip, hesitation flickering across her face like a warning light. "Indirectly. It's . . . a long story. Is there somewhere we can talk?"

My instinct is to say *no*—to protect the house, protect Dad, protect whatever thin safety perimeter I've managed to rebuild in the last few hours. She's a stranger, but she's also Chloe's referral. And something in her eyes tells me she's carrying more fear than threat.

I step aside, gesturing toward the front door. "Sure. Come on in."

She shakes her head, sharply enough that a strand of hair comes loose from her twist. "Not inside," she whispers. "I don't want anyone to overhear us."

A shiver cuts through me—cold, electric, nothing to do with the December air. *Who is this woman afraid of?*

I don't tell her there's no danger inside the house—only my demented father and his caregivers. Because the way she's looking past me—into the trees, toward the road, at the quiet spaces most people don't notice—tells me one thing loud and clear. Whatever she knows didn't stay behind at Willow Creek.

Chapter Seventeen

My mind races as we walk in silence around the side of the house to the backyard. Every instinct I have is screaming that whatever this woman is about to tell me will turn my world upside down. After the scare at the boathouse, I'm half tempted to send her away.

But if my hunches are right, this might be the break in the egg-trafficking case I've been waiting for.

When we reach the patio, Caroline drifts toward the knee wall overlooking the water, admiring the view while I crouch to start a fire in the pit.

"You have a lovely spot," she says softly, turning away from the creek. "Our family has a place on the Corrotoman River, just across the Rappahannock from here."

I nod. "I know it well. We spent a lot of time on the Corrotoman as teenagers. There's a great beach for picnicking at low tide."

She smiles. "Right around the bend from our place."

The flames catch, flickering to life, and Caroline steps closer, rubbing her gloved hands together.

"Would you like some coffee or tea?" I offer. "Our housekeeper makes a delicious spiced chai."

She shakes her head. "I'm fine, thank you." Her gaze shifts past me, through the window, and her expression softens. "Is that your father?"

"Yes, Hollis Sutherlin. He's a retired judge." I'm not sure why I tell her this—maybe because I want her to see the man he was, not the expressionless version sitting frozen beside the fire. "He has Alzheimer's."

A sad smile curves her lips. "I recognize the blank stare. My mother had Alzheimer's. It's such an awful disease. Steals your mind and your dignity. Sometimes she would drift off into these states and stay silent for days."

We barely know each other, and I can't tell her what happened to him this morning—that the blankness isn't from the disease alone but from terror.

"How is Chloe?" I say, treading carefully. While I'm eager to hear her story, I don't want to push. "I spoke to her yesterday morning. She was devastated by the fire."

Caroline presses her lips tight. "We all are. She's looking for another job."

"She mentioned that. After everything that's happened, I don't blame her for distancing herself from the Willow Creek Fertility Clinic."

"I wish I could distance myself from that horrid place." Caroline shivers and pulls her coat tighter around her. "Chloe says you're investigating the fire."

"Among other things." I place a reassuring hand on her arm. "I'd like to hear your story. Whenever you're ready, start at the beginning. Don't leave anything out."

She inhales an unsteady breath, and her green eyes darken—deep as a forest at night, heartbreak buried in the shadows.

"My husband and I tried to conceive for years," she says softly. "Finally, out of desperation, we set up an appointment with Dr. Ellison. After extensive tests, she determined Julian had male-factor infertility. From an old football injury, we think, although we can't be sure." Her voice dips. "He was a proud man, and he struggled with the diagnosis."

My chest tightens. Her use of the past tense confirms what I already suspected. She's the woman Chloe mentioned on the phone yesterday. *Saddest story ever. Her husband died two months ago, and she was scheduled to have their fertilized embryo implanted this morning.*

"I can see how that would be difficult for any man," I mutter, not knowing what else to say.

She nods, eyes fixed on the flames. "But he eventually came around and agreed to IVF. We went through the retrieval process in June—the hormone treatments, the injections, the whole nine yards." A breath trembles out of her. "Ellison told us we had two viable embryos. We did genetic testing—a boy and a girl."

A cold weight sinks into my stomach. Did they name them? All those dreams—an entire future mapped out—shattered in the blink of an eye.

"The day before the transfer, Julian was called to Johns Hopkins to consult on an important case. He was a gifted neurosurgeon. One of the best in the country." She pauses, swallowing. "He left Baltimore at the crack of dawn to make it back in time for the procedure. It was a monumental occasion for us, and he desperately wanted to be here." Her chin trembles. "He fell asleep at the wheel on the interstate and collided head-on with a tractor-trailer."

The air turns heavy, as if even the fire itself bows its head in respect.

Scout presses closer to my leg, sensing the sorrow.

I give Caroline a minute to breathe through the memory.

When she finally continues, her voice is a fragile whisper. "I was devastated. Fortunately, Dr. Ellison had the foresight to freeze the embryos. Two months later, when the fog of grief lifted and I began putting my life back in order, I realized I still had a piece of Julian. *Two* pieces, waiting for me. I scheduled a consultation with Dr. Ellison. She encouraged me to go through with the transfer."

Her breath hitches. "She was murdered the night before my appointment."

My heart cracks clean in half for her. Even though we've only just met, I pull her into my arms. "I'm so sorry. You've had an impossible year."

She nods into my shoulder, fighting back her emotions. When she finally pushes away, she wipes under her eyes and manages, "If you don't mind . . . I'd love that drink now. Water would be great."

I hurry into the kitchen, where Lally stands at the stove. Her long face tells me she's deeply worried about Dad.

She glances over her shoulder as I grab two waters from the fridge. "Who's your friend?"

I let the refrigerator door close. "Just someone I know from Richmond."

"Shall I make you pumpkin spice lattes?"

The kindness in her voice brings tears to my eyes. After this morning's chaos and Caroline's story, I'm already an emotional wreck. Having Lally here feels like a lifeline. I throw my arms around her. "Thank you. That would be lovely."

She pats my back, startled but smiling.

I step away, wiping under my eyes. "Better add a splash of Baileys. We both need it."

I return to the patio to find Caroline seated in a lounge chair, eyes lost somewhere over the water, her hand absently scratching Scout's head.

"Careful," I say, handing her a water. "She'll never leave your side. She's loyal to anyone who gives her attention . . . or food. Mostly food."

Caroline laughs. "She reminds me of the yellow lab I had growing up. What's her name?"

"Scout. Our housekeeper is making us pumpkin spice lattes. She should be out soon."

"That's so nice. Thank you." Caroline unscrews the cap and takes a long swallow. "There's still so much to tell you, Lane. I feel bad for barging in unannounced and taking up so much of your time."

"Not at all. I have nowhere I need to be. And truthfully, I'm at a standstill in my investigation, and you may have the clues I need to move forward." I sit beside her, the fire warming my face. "So . . . I assume Ellison's death delayed your transfer."

Caroline grimaces. "Yes. That's correct. The clinic was in complete turmoil after she was murdered. Ellison ran the show. Without her, none of the other doctors seemed to know which itch to scratch."

She settles back in her chair. "I'd gotten to know Chloe during my appointments with Dr. Ellison. When I called her for a referral, we ended up talking for a long time. She confided in me about missing patient charts . . . and missing eggs."

Caroline lifts one shoulder. "Honestly, she probably said more than she should have, but she knew I'd just lost my husband. She was trying to help." Her expression tightens with the memory. "She dug through my chart personally, making certain my embryos were still safely stored in the lab. Then, she rearranged Dr. Kincaid's schedule so he could see me right away."

"Kincaid," I say softly, filing the name away in my memory. "When was this?"

"The last week in September." Caroline's finger shoots up. "But this is where it gets even more interesting. The morning before my appointment, I overheard a discussion between two women at my yoga class. They were talking about black-market eggs and embryos—the higher the quality, the more expensive."

I sit up straighter. This is proof of everything I feared. "I'm sorry . . . what?"

She nods, eyes widening slightly. "Can you believe it? They were chatting like it was the latest wellness trend. Comparing it to ordering a luxury car—everything customizable. One of them even bragged about *designing* a genius child."

My mouth falls open, but no words tumble out.

"I know. It's mind-boggling. After class, I followed one of

them out to the parking lot. When I asked her to elaborate on their discussion, she brushed it off. Then she gave me that look I've grown to detest—pity disguised as kindness." Caroline's mouth firms into a grief-sharpened line. "She said that black-market sourcing might be a good option for me now that I was widowed. Can you believe that?"

"Nothing surprises me anymore, Caroline. Did she say anything else?"

"Only that I should reach out to Dr. Kincaid at Willow Creek Fertility."

I shake my head, somber. "This is all so bizarre."

"Tell me about it. I mentioned the conversation casually to Dr. Kincaid when I went for my appointment the next day. His whole demeanor shifted—like someone had pulled a wire inside him too tight. He mumbled something about not getting sucked into gossip."

I lean forward. "What a jerk. I hope you walked out of there."

Caroline drains the last of her water. "As tempted as I was, I couldn't. I needed him for the IVF. My transfer was rescheduled for yesterday."

My skin crawls. "Then the lab caught fire—"

Caroline's voice cracks as she finishes for me. "And someone stole my embryos."

My ears perk. *Stole?* "I don't mean to be insensitive, but how can you be sure they weren't destroyed in the fire?"

Her eyes meet mine. "I have no proof, but it makes sense when you think about it. The lab was the vault. And whoever did this took the jewels, then torched the place to hide the empty shelves."

"Oh my God. I was right. They didn't burn the lab to destroy records—to erase databases or hide paperwork. This is grand larceny—only the stolen property wasn't jewelry or cash. It was human life."

A prickle races up the back of my neck. I turn. Judd stands in the doorway, three steaming mugs trembling in his hands, his face pale and eyes locked on me like he's seeing something he can't unsee.

"How long have you been standing there?" I ask.

"Long enough." He looks at Caroline, then back at me. "You're not just talking about grand larceny."

A beat.

"You're talking about kidnapping."

Chapter Eighteen

Judd steps down to the patio, handing each of us a mug. "Sounds like we're going to need more than one shot of Baileys. Should I bring out the whole bottle?"

I choke out an awkward laugh. "Caroline, this is my brother, Judd."

She offers him a polite smile. "Nice to meet you."

"Same. Although I wish the circumstances were different." His voice is full of compassion. "I'm sorry about your missing embabies."

I blink. "Your what? I've never heard that term. Did you just make it up?"

Judd rolls his eyes. "Um . . . no."

Caroline's mouth curves sadly. "It's a legitimate term, although most doctors don't approve of it. Em-babies—fertilized embryos we're hoping will become our babies."

My head swivels back to Judd. "How'd you hear it?"

"My wife's expecting," he explains to Caroline. "She knows a lot about fertility. We tried for over a year to get pregnant." His voice softens. "I know a little about what you're going through."

Caroline's smile fades. "It's been a rough time."

Judd turns to me then—not angry but clearly shaken. "Are

you investigating egg trafficking now? Does this have something to do with the Craddocks?"

"Excuse us," I murmur to Caroline.

I grab Judd's arm and guide him out into the yard. "Listen, Judd," I whisper. "Your wife is pregnant. You're about to be a father. You need to keep your distance from my investigation—and from the Craddocks."

He jerks his arm free. "I'm already involved, Lane. We're all living here together—one big happy family commune." His voice softens. "Tell me what you need. Whatever it is . . . I'm in." His gaze flicks back to Caroline. "That poor woman lost her future children."

A slow sigh escapes me. "You probably missed the part about Caroline's husband being killed in a car accident. Those *embabies* aren't just her future children. They're her last pieces of him—a boy and a girl."

Judd's face falls, his expression wounded. Fatherhood has softened him in a good way.

"I have reason to believe the Craddocks are neck-deep in this," I continue. "And you know how dangerous they are. You saw what they did to Dad this morning. I'd never forgive myself if anything happened to Brandy . . . or to you."

His jaw tightens. "The sooner we deal with them, the better."

My brother's stance is rigid, his scowl determined. It's over. There's no pulling him back now.

"Fine," I mutter. "But I'm in charge. And you're on a need-to-know basis." I jerk my chin toward the kitchen. "Now go get the Baileys bottle."

When the door closes behind him, I return to the fire, stoking the logs before adding several more on top. I drop into my chair. "He's staying for now. And honestly? He might actually help. He knows a lot more about what goes on in this town than me."

Tears well in her eyes. "I'll take all the help I can get."

Judd returns with the Baileys bottle, handing it to me before sitting down across from us.

I add a splash to my mug and straighten. "All right. If we all put our heads together, maybe we can make sense of what we already know."

Caroline wipes her cheek. Judd leans forward. Both waiting for me.

I take a breath. "Caroline, earlier you mentioned quality affects value. According to Chloe, many of the clinic's patients are high profile—wives and daughters of politicians, people with serious influence. That sort of thing. Do your embryos fall into that . . . so-called high-value category?"

She drops her gaze. "My husband was a brilliant neurosurgeon. Truly gifted. His IQ was off the charts." She hesitates. "And I have a different type of aptitude. I've been able to play music by ear since I was a small child. I'm a musical savant, a concert pianist."

My brow lifts. "That definitely sheds new light on things." I sip my latte, pausing a minute to think. "Given the circumstances, do you think your embryos were specifically targeted? Ellison's death prevented your first transfer. The fire prevented your second. That's a little too close to be random."

"Actually . . ." Her voice wavers. "There were three delays. My husband's fatal car accident interfered with the first." She presses her fingers to her temples, like the thought physically hurts. "What if it wasn't an accident?"

I wouldn't put it past the Craddocks. Addie's spreadsheets show the obscene prices high-quality eggs fetch on the black market. But this woman has already endured enough. She doesn't need her husband's death dragging her under too.

"Whatever happened is in the past," I say gently. "The most important thing now is finding your embryos . . . your embabies. Have you spoken to the authorities?"

"Only Detective McDermott."

I groan inwardly. Why do all roads lead to Milo? "When was this?"

"Yesterday, at the scene of the fire. He wasn't much help. He laughed when I told him my theory—that my embryos were taken before the fire. That the fire was used to cover the traffickers' tracks."

So Milo knows Caroline's onto them. Her shiny black Range Rover is impossible to miss. If Shadow Man is stationed in his usual spot at the end of our drive, he saw her arrive. It won't take long for them to put two and two together. Word will get back to Milo. If her embryos are worth as much as I think they are, he'll kill her to prevent her from getting them back.

"You seemed on edge when you first pulled up," I say carefully. "Is there something else you haven't told us?"

She bites her lower lip. "I'm pretty sure someone is following me."

I exchange a look with my brother.

He beats me to the punch. "Where are you staying, Caroline?"

A flush creeps up her neck. "I'm . . . not sure, honestly. I brought some clothes. I could stay at our place on the Corrotoman, but it's remote. The closest neighbor is miles away."

Judd's hand shoots out, decisive. "You'll stay here with us. My wife and I are living in the guest cottage right now, but there are plenty of rooms in the main house."

Caroline immediately shakes her head. "Oh, no—I couldn't. I've already troubled you enough."

"You may be in danger. You shouldn't be alone." He turns to me. "Lane? You okay with that?"

I study him—this unexpectedly protective version of my brother I barely recognize.

I give an enthusiastic nod. "Absolutely, I'm okay with that. In fact, I insist. You're safer here with us—at least for a couple of days, until I can track down some of these new leads."

The French door swings open, and Lally bellows, "Lunch!"

A laugh escapes me. "There it is. The final verdict. You're staying."

Caroline smiles. "In that case, I accept your offer."

Our commune is growing. Our guns are cleaned. The alarm's

updated. The house is as close to a fortress as we can make it. For now.

Caroline sits next to Dad at lunch. She talks to him like she's known him forever—gentle questions, quiet comments, a running thread of soft humor—and even though he meets her with silence, something in him shifts. His shoulders ease. His gaze softens.

"I'm a musician," she tells him. "A pianist. Am I right in pegging you for a classical music fan?"

A faint smile tugs at his lips, the first I've seen since the ordeal at the boathouse.

When I tell him Caroline will be staying with us for a while, he gives the slightest nod of approval, as though she's already earned a spot in his shrinking world.

Lunch is simple—ham biscuits, homemade beef vegetable soup, a platter of sliced apples—but Caroline treats it like a feast, thanking Lally so earnestly that Lally blushes. It's the first time I've ever seen Lally blush.

After we eat, Judd helps haul Caroline's luggage upstairs before heading back to work—promising to bring home steaks for dinner.

I eye her small mountain of designer suitcases. "Are you planning to be gone a while?"

She lets out a breathy laugh. "I was in such a hurry, I just started throwing things in." She pulls a cashmere scarf from one bag and loops it around her neck. "I feel better . . . somehow lighter . . . now that I'm here. I didn't realize how much I needed to get away. Staying cooped up in that house with my husband's ghost was taking a toll on me."

"Do you go on tour often?"

"I used to. A lot." She strokes the scarf fringe absently. "But it's been years, and I'm out of practice. I'm not sure anyone would even book me now."

I test the doorknob of the guest room, making sure the lock catches. "Keep this locked at night. Dad wanders sometimes. He won't hurt you, but he may show up in your doorway at two a.m. thinking he's looking for his chambers at the courthouse."

She laughs softly. "He seems sweet. Mom had the ugly version of Alzheimer's—she could turn mean in the blink of an eye. Chased off more than one caregiver." She takes her cosmetic bag into the adjoining bathroom. When she returns, she asks, "Is there a pattern to his wandering?"

I frown. "I'm not sure what you mean. He waits until no one is watching, then leaves the house."

Caroline nods gently. "People with Alzheimer's sometimes wander for a reason. They may feel afraid of their surroundings and try to escape. Or they're searching for someone familiar. Or they're attempting to get somewhere their mind tells them they're supposed to be." She hesitates. "Does it usually happen at night? Or after he's been sleeping?"

A vision flashes—Dad standing at the French doors in nothing but his underwear, eyes vacant and frightened after a nap.

"Not always at night. But usually after he's been asleep. He wakes up disoriented . . . like he's stepped out of a different reality."

I sag against the doorjamb as the realization hits. "And sometimes, during these spells, he talks about my oldest brother, Tommy. Nonsense, mostly. But it's always Tommy. He died in a boating accident nineteen years ago."

Caroline's expression softens. "I'm no expert, but maybe he's trying to find Tommy. Or . . . maybe something about that accident still haunts him, and this is how his mind is trying to make sense of it. Grief leaves long shadows. Maybe he's still trying to walk through his."

"Maybe."

Through the window, my gaze follows the creek toward Oyster Bay and the Rappahannock River—the place Tommy vanished from our lives forever. There are things about that accident I've never fully understood either. But as the autumn light streams through the blinds, a quiet certainty settles into my bones: some truths don't want to stay buried.

Chapter Nineteen

Leaving Caroline to get settled, I retreat to my corner of the breakfast table. Scout curls at my feet and a few snowflakes drift lazily past the window as the house slips into its midafternoon quiet. I open my laptop, fall down the Colt Craddock rabbit hole, and hit bottom faster than expected.

For a man from one of Tidewell's most powerful families, Colt Craddock barely exists online. No LinkedIn. No Facebook or Instagram. No employment records, no professional affiliations. Nothing that explains how he spends his days—or why he works so hard to conceal them.

I manage to dig up two photos—one from a wildlife fundraiser, another from Tidewell's annual turkey trot. Both taken from a distance. No tags. No captions. No quotes. He's present but never quite *there*.

I broaden the search—court records, archived news articles, property filings. Still nothing. Not even a speeding ticket. No real estate in his name until three years ago when he inherited his family's hundred-acre estate.

Google Earth finds it instantly. The Overlook. The registered historic site was once home to Colonel Edmund Ashcroft, a prominent Virginia planter and shipping magnate. Built in the early

1800s, the brick Georgian house sits high above the river—central block flanked by wings, a long drive disappearing beneath a canopy of old-growth trees.

From above, it looks serene. Red brick glowing against manicured lawns, the river stretching wide and calm below. From a distance, it's exactly what it claims to be—historic, preserved, untouchable.

I toggle to 3D view and let the property rotate. That's when I see it. Beyond the main house, near the tree line, sits a long, low outbuilding, a barn or carriage house. The roof is dark with age, the structure half swallowed by brush. Abandoned at first glance. But the driveway leading to it is freshly graveled. Whatever it once was, someone is using it now.

I move on to his son. My quick search of Colter Craddock uncovers exactly what I expected. Recent UVA graduate. No LinkedIn—meaning no professional ambition worth advertising. No employment records. No paper trail beyond his diploma.

His Instagram, on the other hand, is thriving. Thousands of followers. A feed stuffed with hunting kills, fishing trophies, and shirtless photos on boats—every image screaming rugged masculinity, none of them attached to anything that resembles work.

Colter is the kind of man who wants to be feared. Colt is the kind who actually is.

I lean back in the chair and watch as the computer screen fades to black. I've tracked criminals across state lines. I've dug into the backgrounds of people who deliberately torched their pasts and built new lives from the ashes. But Colt Craddock isn't reinventing anything. He's erasing. And the silence around him speaks volumes.

I text Morales.

Get me everything you can find on Colt Craddock. He's covering his tracks online.

He replies instantly.

On it.

I'm organizing my screenshots when music from the out-of-tune baby grand piano drifts down the hallway. Soft at first—like the house itself is humming. Classical. Familiar. A melody that aches as much as it comforts.

I push back from the table and follow the sound to the front living room.

Caroline is perched at the piano, framed by the living room window, afternoon light warming the dark shine of her hair. Her fingers move with effortless fluency—velvet one moment, lightning the next—coaxing something old and beautiful from the ivory keys. A piece that carries both grief and hope.

Dad sits on the nearby sofa, swaying ever so gently, his eyes soft and misty—the most lucid I've seen him all day. Even Scout seems spellbound, head in her paws, tail thumping quietly in rhythm.

I rest my shoulder against the doorjamb and close my eyes. For a moment, the world narrows to the music . . . the warmth . . . the fragile peace of it all.

Caroline was right about Dad. I grew up on a steady diet of Mozart, Beethoven, and Tchaikovsky—his holy trinity. Most nights, he'd fill the house with symphonies loud enough to rattle the windows, insisting it sharpened the mind.

For the first time in a long time, the house doesn't feel hollowed out by fear and loss. It feels . . . full. Renewed. Like all those autumn evenings of my childhood when my brothers and I tumbled through the back door after sports practice and found Dad in the kitchen, wooden spoon in hand, conducting his imaginary orchestra while sautéing onions and over-salting everything in sight.

I watch Dad watching Caroline. He's spellbound, caught in a moment of clarity I wish I could hold still. A tight ache blooms behind my ribs. Music reaches him in a place I can't anymore. I'm grateful for that, even as it hurts.

Caroline has done the impossible. She's pulled him out of the catatonic fog that swallowed him after the traumatic events in the boathouse this morning. And I like her all the more for it.

Briggs's accusation flickers through my mind—*I think all women intimidate you.*

That's not it. That's never been it. I'm not threatened by other women. I just don't click with most of them. Maybe that's my fault.

But Caroline is different. She's real and intelligent and gracious without trying to impress anyone. Despite her obvious wealth, there's not a hint of pretense in her. If I had a girl squad, Caroline would make the cut.

I clap when the music ends. "Bravo."

Caroline bows her head with understated elegance. "It's nice to have an audience again." She glances toward the window, where fat flakes of snow drift past the glass. "I realize it's not yet Thanksgiving, but the weather is making me feel festive."

Her fingers return to the keys, featherlight, and the room blooms with the opening chords of "White Christmas."

I move to the sofa beside Dad. For the next hour, she carries us through a winter concert—jazz arrangements, bright playful pieces, and solemn classical carols that seem to hush the entire house. Dad stays alert the whole time, his gaze fixed on her hands like he's rediscovered something precious.

But when the final note fades, he rises without a word and shuffles off to his study.

Caroline catches the flicker of worry in my expression. "He just needs a little time," she says softly. "Moments like that can take a lot out of someone—even the good ones."

Dusk has settled into the corners of the room, and I switch on the lamp on the table beside me. I check my phone—six o'clock already? Lally and Shawna must've slipped out during the performance.

I slowly get up from the sofa, hating to leave the comfort of the cozy room. "Judd will be home any minute with the steaks. I should get dinner going."

Caroline lowers the cover on the keys. "I'll help. I can make a potato casserole if you'd like."

"That sounds perfect. I'll throw together a spinach salad. I don't know about you, but I could use a glass of wine right about now."

"Oh, yes! Please," Caroline says, stepping in line beside me as we head to the kitchen.

I retrieve a bottle from Dad's cellar, and we sip red wine while we work.

Judd arrives home thirty minutes later. "Here are the steaks," he says, dropping the grocery bag on the counter. He spots the open bottle and pours himself a generous glass.

Something in his expression is off—pale around the edges, jaw tight. But I wait until Caroline excuses herself to freshen up before asking. "What's up, bro? I can tell something's troubling you."

Judd exhales sharply. "I had my first run-in with the Night Ryders a few minutes ago."

I freeze, hand hovering over the salad bowl. "What happened?"

"Their little parade of black pickups was lined up across the Publix parking lot when I came out of the store." He rubs the back of his neck, irritated and unsettled. "I've never even met Colter Craddock, but he sure as hell knew my name. Walked right up to me. Threatened me—right there in the middle of the parking lot. Told me to watch my back and to keep my sister in line." Judd snorts. "I felt like a kid again, being bullied on the playground by the biggest idiot in the class."

I can't help the laugh that slips out. "An accurate description. But I'm sorry he's picking on you because of me." I unwrap the steaks from the butcher paper and arrange them on a platter. "I hope they're not picking on Brandy. Have you checked on her today?"

"Yeah." He sprinkles seasoning on the steaks with a heavy hand. "I stopped by the cottage on my way here. She's not eating with us—morning sickness is winning today."

"I'm sorry she's miserable."

He shrugs. "Me too. But it's a good sign the pregnancy is progressing."

I fold my arms, studying him. "Tell me more about the Craddocks."

Judd exhales. "Same old story. Spoiled little rich boys with no consequences. Colt and Wylie lost their mother when they were young, and their father let them run wild. He bailed them out of every stupid stunt and covered up the rest."

"Why did their father leave The Overlook to Colt alone? Did he cut Wylie out of the will entirely?"

Judd shrugs without looking at me. "I have no idea, Laney. And I don't much care. They're entitled, rich little pricks. And the way things are going . . ." He sets down the seasoning so hard it rattles the counter. "They'll end up owning this town, and we'll all be at their mercy."

A chill runs through me. He's not just annoyed anymore—he's afraid. "What aren't you telling me?"

He stares at the steaks, but he's not seeing them. "Wylie Craddock has already killed someone in this family."

My blood runs cold. He's talking about Tommy. "Don't go there, Judd."

His head lifts, eyes haunted. "I can't stop thinking about it. Tom didn't fall off that damn boat. He handled a boat better than half the captains on the bay. And despite what people whispered, he wasn't drunk. He wasn't a drinker."

"What makes you so sure?"

Judd swipes a hand through his hair. "Tom and Wylie were fighting on the beach earlier that day. Nobody knows what the fight was about. And one of them isn't alive to explain." A muscle ticks along his jaw. "There is more to the accident than we were told."

"Maybe you're right. But how do we prove something that happened nineteen years ago?"

"You're the detective. That's your job." He takes a sip of wine. "Not now. You've got enough on your plate. But once we find Caroline's embryos, you and I are going to deep dive that accident."

"Are you sure you want to open that can of worms?" I ask quietly.

He nods, meeting my eyes with a fierce finality that steals my breath. "I have to know, Laney. I can't live the rest of my life wondering what happened to Tom. And if Wylie Craddock had anything to do with it . . ." His voice roughens. "I'll make damn sure he pays for it."

Chapter Twenty

Nightmares about Tommy plague my sleep Thursday night —one bleeding into the next until I can't tell waking from dreaming. I bolt upright before dawn on Friday, lungs tight, heart racing, adrenaline already burning through my veins. It's the kind of restless energy that has a history of getting me into trouble.

And yet, for the first time in nineteen years, I'm ready to dig into the past. Ready to face whatever truth is buried beneath the wreckage of Tommy's death and everything that came after.

But slow is the only way forward. Too much is at stake now. Every move must be calculated—tactical. Caroline is counting on me to find her embryos, and if I make one wrong move, the Craddocks won't just bury the past. They'll bury us too.

Over coffee an hour later, I inform Caroline of my decision to go to Richmond today. "I want to see this Dr. Kincaid in person. Will you be okay here until I get back?"

A flicker of uncertainty crosses her face. "I'll be fine. Don't worry about me. Are you sure you know what you're doing?"

Her question feels like an insult. Then I remind myself she doesn't really know me. "Yes, Caroline. I'm a professional. I know what I'm doing."

Sliding off the barstool, I rinse my coffee mug and place it in the dishwasher. "Lally and Shawna will be here all day," I reassure her. "And Judd works in town—only fifteen minutes away. If anything feels off, call him."

She nods, her shoulders sagging. "I may spend the day practicing. The piano helps settle my nerves."

I smile at her. "Dad will be thrilled to give you an audience."

"Do you have an appointment with Dr. Kincaid?" Caroline asks.

I shake my head. "But I'm not worried. He'll see me."

I pat my hip for the familiar weight of my gun. "I should get going."

Caroline walks me to the mudroom, Scout trotting faithfully at her side—like she's already switched allegiances. "Be careful, Lane. These are dangerous people."

"I will." I slip on my coat and toss my bag over my shoulder. I open the back door, slapping my thigh to get Scout's attention. "Come on, girl. You're riding shotgun."

Scout doesn't move. She sits at attention, leaning slightly into Caroline's leg.

Caroline's mouth quirks. "I think she wants to keep me company."

A tiny, ridiculous sting prickles my skin. "Traitor," I mutter under my breath.

Scout gives me a single thump of her tail—as if to say *you'll live*.

I lean over to pet her. "All right, then. You're in charge of protecting the house. And everyone in it."

Caroline's expression shifts. I can't read it—gratitude, worry, or something much deeper. "Stay in touch," she murmurs. "Whatever you do, be sure to come back."

"I always do."

But as the brisk morning air hits my face, a knot tightens low in my stomach. I can feel it in my bones—Tidewell's about to ignite, and I'm walking straight into the fire.

Instead of heading toward town, I take a left and drive deeper into the country. Shadow Man picks up my trail immediately, pulling in behind me without the slightest bit of subtlety.

I tighten my grip on the wheel and let my speed drift five miles over the limit. He matches it.

I drop back to the speed limit. So does he.

He's sticking close enough to keep me in sight but far enough to pretend he's not tailing me. *Amateur hour.*

I nudge the accelerator again—ten over this time—letting the distance stretch just enough to bait him. He takes it, closing the gap until he's riding my bumper, locking me in his sights.

The next bend hands me exactly what I'm waiting for: a narrow turnoff swallowed by pines, nothing more than a forgotten access road locals use for deer season. Outsiders never notice it.

At the last possible second, I ease off the gas, crank the wheel, and slip into the cut. Gravel spits under my tires as the trees swallow me whole.

Shadow Man's black Chevy blasts past, none the wiser.

Keeping low behind the line of cedar and pine, I roll forward until the dirt trail spits me out onto the highway toward West Point.

Richmond, here I come.

I wait until I'm passing through West Point to call the clinic. The receptionist tells me in a clipped, sugary tone that Dr. Kincaid is booked solid all morning. I leave an urgent message requesting a call back.

Thirty minutes later, when I've heard nothing from him, I call again.

Same receptionist. The sweetness is gone, replaced by open irritation. "I already told you, Dr. Kincaid is unavailable."

"This is urgent police business concerning the fire at the lab," I explain, voice calm. "I'll be at the clinic in forty-five minutes. I expect to speak with him then."

A long, dramatic sigh. "Give me your contact information."

"I gave it to you thirty minutes ago."

"Oops," she says flatly. "I must have thrown it in the trash."

My jaw ticks as I repeat my number. "This time, don't throw it away." I hang up before she can respond.

Three minutes later, my phone rings from an unknown number. I answer on the first ring. "Detective Sutherlin."

Laurence Kincaid's voice is low and strained. "Meet me at the Palmer Chapel Mausoleum in Hollywood Cemetery in thirty minutes."

My pulse jumps. *Hollywood Cemetery.* "I can make that work."

"I'll be seated on a bench overlooking the water. You will *not* sit. Stand beside me as if we're strangers. Speak quietly." He pauses a split second. "And, Detective . . . make certain you aren't followed."

As the line goes dead, chill bumps skate up my arms. Whatever game Kincaid is playing, it just veered into dangerous territory.

I stare at my phone, replaying his instructions. A public cemetery. A mausoleum. Don't sit. Don't act familiar. Make sure I'm not followed.

Why hide a meeting from his own staff? Two possibilities form like storm fronts colliding. Either he's being threatened . . . or he's part of the threat. Maybe someone's leaning on him—the power behind the egg trafficking. Maybe he refused to play in their sandbox, and now he's spooked. Or maybe he's neck-deep in their embryo heist and terrified I'll sniff it out.

None of these options feel good.

Whatever Kincaid knows, he's scared enough to risk meeting me in a graveyard. Which means what he has to say is either incriminating . . . or dangerous as hell.

The cemetery sprawls across 135 acres of rolling hills and deep-cut valleys, its winding roads shadowed by towering oaks and ancient magnolias. The place feels suspended in time—quiet, heavy, watchful. No sign of boogeymen. Just a few scattered families tending graves, their voices hushed by the cold morning air.

To be certain I wasn't followed, I park near Presidents Circle—

final resting place of Presidents James Monroe and John Tyler—and take the footpath down toward the mausoleum.

I spot him from a distance—seated alone on an iron bench overlooking the James River. A dark cashmere overcoat drapes over his slightly stooped shoulders, as if the weight he's carrying isn't just the fabric. A felt hat—dark brown, brim low—shields most of his face, and a red plaid scarf is knotted neatly at his throat, bright against the muted gray of the morning.

Wind tunnels through the mausoleum as I pass through the chapel, stinging my face and hands. This early cold front is uncharacteristic for Virginia in November—an omen of the long, punishing months ahead.

Kincaid doesn't turn as I approach. I stand beside him for a beat before breaking the silence. "Nice view."

He nods once. "I come here to visit my wife." He pauses a beat. "What do you want, Sutherlin?"

I'd anticipated the question. I don't hesitate. "The truth."

He lets out a humorless huff. "Then you're already out of step with the rest of your pals in law enforcement."

"Maybe so. But I'm doing everything in my power to remedy that." I shift my weight, pulling my jacket tighter. "Are you being threatened? Is someone following you? Do you need protection?"

"And if I say yes?" His eyes stay on the water. "Who exactly would you ask for that protection? Detective McDermott?"

Milo's name slaps me in the face like the wind whipping off the river.

"Milo McDermott is not the only option," I say evenly. "I *can* help you, Dr. Kincaid. But you have to tell me everything."

His jaw hardens. "I won't take the fall for Dr. Ellison. She made her bed. As of today, I'm done carrying the weight of it." He lifts his coffee, taking a slow sip. "She came to me the night before she was killed. She confessed her sob story. I felt sorry for her at the time." His mouth tightens. "Now, I wish I'd sent her away."

"That kind of regret usually comes too late. What was she mixed up in?"

"A few years back, her husband spiraled into gambling debt. She reached out to an old friend from medical school. She was just looking for a loan. Instead, she got herself entangled in something she couldn't walk away from."

"Who was the college friend she reached out to? Did she give you a name?"

He snorts softly. "No. Just said it was someone she once trusted. And honestly? I'm glad I didn't push her for more. If I had . . . I might not be talking to you right now."

He finally turns his head, just enough to glance at me. His eyes are sharp despite their weariness. "She sold patient eggs and embryos for obscene amounts of money." His lip curls. "Despicable. Maybe she didn't deserve to die for it, but she definitely should've lost her medical license."

"I agree," I say quietly. "Why did she come to you? Was she in danger?"

"Yes. She wanted out. Her husband had cleaned himself up, and she no longer needed the money. But her college friend and his colleagues needed her. They call themselves the Harvesters. Fitting . . . and chilling. People who treat women's bodies like crops to be picked clean." He coughs into a gloved hand. "Anyway, the Harvesters weren't about to lose their golden goose. So she went to the police." He lifts a hand, as if to say, *What else could she do*? "She told Detective McDermott everything she knew."

The thought turns my stomach. "Did McDermott investigate?" I ask, even though I already know the answer.

Kincaid's mouth twists. "He investigated all right. Investigated himself right into the middle of the trafficking ring. The Harvesters don't dirty their hands. They leave that to the Reaper. In this case, the Reaper is McDermott."

I knew Milo McDermott was dirty. I had no idea how filthy. "How many people are in this organization?"

He hunches a shoulder. "I can't say for sure."

"If this goes to trial," I say carefully, "would you be willing to testify against Detective McDermott?"

His fingers tense around the coffee cup. "As long as everyone in the organization is behind bars."

"Were you aware someone tampered with the surveillance cameras outside the lab prior to the fire?"

He lifts his head slowly, eyes narrowing beneath the brim of his felt hat. "I was not. But I'm not surprised. It fits my theory."

My pulse kicks. "What theory is that? That the fire was a cover-up—that the Harvesters removed the eggs and embryos *before* they set the blaze?"

He gives a single, tight nod. "But you didn't hear that from me."

"You have my word." I hesitate. "How difficult would it be to transport the goods?"

His eyes return to the river. "Not difficult at all. Nitrogen-charged transport tanks are readily available. They are used every day for legitimate medical transfers. All you need is access and someone who knows how to handle them."

I sense his patience thinning, the air between us tightening. "What do you know about Caroline Edwards?"

He doesn't hesitate. "She's a lovely young woman who's been dealt a cruel hand. I assume you've met her?"

"Yes, sir. She believes her embryos were stolen. She enlisted me to find them. If her embryos were part of the heist, is it possible they're still viable?"

"Possible. And likely." His voice drops. "McDermott expressed particular interest in her embryos. Her husband was a brilliant surgeon. She's a gifted musician. Those embryos would fetch a very high price on the black market."

"I repeat my question from earlier. Do you need protection, Dr. Kincaid?"

"No. The only way out of this—for me—is retirement." His shoulders sag. "I'm ready. I don't understand the world anymore."

"Neither do I, Doctor." I draw a steady breath. "One last thing. Where did Dr. Ellison attend medical school?"

"Duke." He rises slowly from the bench to face me. "You're sworn to uphold the law, Detective. I hope—for both our sakes—you still mean it."

"Oh, I mean it." I hold his gaze. "This is a battle of good versus evil on more than one front. And too many roads lead back to your lab. I'll do whatever I can to bring down the Harvesters."

I extend my hand, and he grips it firmly.

"Good luck, Detective. You're going to need it."

Chapter Twenty-One

I drive slow loops around the cemetery, trying to make sense of everything Kincaid just told me. I can easily see how Milo got pulled in—he'd sell his soul to the devil for a dollar. Ellison's old college friend is the missing piece. Find him—or her—and we've got the ringleader.

If the Craddock brothers are involved—and all signs point that way—what do they know about harvesting eggs? Neither Colt nor Wylie are doctors. They may have medical degrees, but they aren't practicing physicians. And even if transporting embryos isn't difficult, someone with experience in cryogenic storage must handle them. I can't imagine them trusting something as volatile as human eggs to just anyone.

I'm circling toward the cemetery exit when Morales calls. "Can you talk?"

"Yep. I'm alone in my car, leaving Hollywood Cemetery."

"You're in Richmond?" His surprise carries a faint edge, like I'm supposed to log my whereabouts with him.

"Ten-four. I just left Dr. Kincaid." I pass the cemetery office and through the stone columns.

"Ah . . . Ellison's partner. Did you learn anything worth sharing?"

"Tidbits. Enough to create a lot of new questions. If you want, I can stop by the station on my way out of town?"

"Better yet, meet me at Starbucks in Carytown. Thirty minutes."

"Got it. See you in a few."

I make a left toward the interstate and drive the short distance to the Cary Street exit.

At Starbucks, I order an espresso and grab a small table in a corner. I'm scrolling through emails when Morales plops down in the chair opposite me, Starbucks cup in hand.

I look up from my phone. "Hey, Sarge."

"Hey, yourself." He studies my face. "Still got that haunted look in your eyes."

I let out a huff. "I don't think it's going anywhere, anytime soon."

He plants his elbows on the table. "So—where are we? Tell me about your meeting with Kincaid."

I lean in. "The doctor and I are on the same page about one thing. We both believe the cryogenic tanks were emptied—the eggs and embryos stolen—before the fire started."

His brow knits. "That explains why the surveillance cameras went down and the footage was wiped. Do you have any other evidence to back up your claim?"

"I'm working on it." I tug on my lower lip. "There's something else you should know. A young woman came to me for help— Caroline Edwards. Her embryos were taken—embryos fertilized by her late husband's sperm. Needless to say, she wants them back. And because we have no way of knowing if they're being properly stored, time is of the essence."

"Are we talking about Caroline Edwards, the concert pianist?"

I nod. "Do you know her?"

"Her husband saved my cousin's life—extracted a tumor from her brain when other doctors said it couldn't be done. His death was tragic. I know little about Caroline, other than she's a gifted pianist."

"She's a remarkable person. You'd like her. If we don't move fast, someone will sell her embryos to the highest bidder."

Morales rubs his temples, his face grim. "I'm having a difficult time wrapping my mind around this case. It's all just so . . . unimaginable."

"Try wrapping your mind around this." I don't sugarcoat what comes next. "Milo's involved in the egg trafficking up to his receding hairline. They call him the Reaper. He does their dirty work. Kincaid's willing to testify against him, but only after we dismantle the operation."

The truth lands heavy. I can see it in his eyes. But he doesn't push back. His silence tells me he's already doing the math.

I take the next few minutes to fill him in on my conversation with Kincaid. When I tell him about Ellison teaming up with an old college friend from Duke, he bolts upright, rattling the table.

"Colt Craddock attended Duke. I'm still confirming dates, but I'd bet my life he overlapped with Ellison. And get this—he was forced out after he was busted selling cadaver parts on the black market."

"Bingo." I lean back in my chair, the picture finally snapping into place. "Let me guess. Daddy Dearest had those records sealed."

Morales fires a finger gun at me. "Care to guess Colt's current occupation?" He doesn't wait for me to respond. "He runs a biomedical courier service—MidAtlantic BioLogistics."

My mouth actually falls open.

Morales grins. "Careful, Sutherlin. You might catch a fly."

I shake my head, baffled. "Let me get this straight. Colt gets expelled for selling cadaver parts, pivots into a *legitimate* business hauling medical specimens, and uses the exact same expertise to traffic embryos. That's not a career change—that's a rebrand."

"Pretty much." Morales's grin fades. "So, we've got the what and the how. Now all we need is the where." He strokes his beard stubble. "I'd put my money on a northeastern city. Major hub. Easier distribution."

"That's one possibility." I stare up at the ceiling, lost in thought, drumming my fingers on the table.

I can feel Morales watching me. "What're you thinking, Sutherlin?"

"What if it's happening right under our noses? Colt recently inherited his family's estate—a hundred acres twenty miles from Tidewell on the Rappahannock River. Middle of nowhere. On Google Earth, I saw a new gravel road leading to an older structure on the property."

He nods slowly. "You might be onto something. Have you seen Colt around town?"

"Yep. He tried to pick me up at Slip 99 the other night. And I saw him with his son—and your number one detective, Milo—at the Tide House at the crack of dawn yesterday morning."

Morales narrows his eyes. "What's the Tide House?"

"An old watermen's boathouse in Founders Park. And before you ask why I was there at dawn, I was walking my dog." I hold my gaze steady, not breaking eye contact as the lie slips from my lips. Morales is a friend of Dad's. He knows about the Alzheimer's. But I'd rather not put Hollis's worst moments on the record.

"When'd you get a dog?" Morales asks.

"She belonged to Addie. Let's just say we found each other after her death." I push back from the table. "I need a drone. Any ideas?"

Morales gives me a suspicious look. "What are you planning, Sutherlin?"

"A stakeout at The Overlook. Can you get me a drone?"

He goes quiet for a beat, weighing the cost of helping me. "I have one in my trunk, actually. Along with a few other pieces of equipment that might come in handy."

I arch a brow. "Why do you have that kind of gear in your trunk? Did your *go bag* get an upgrade?"

He chuckles. "Something like that. I attended a conference

recently. Vendors were showing off their new toys. I grabbed a few swag items—strictly for educational purposes."

I roll my eyes. "Yeah, right. You and your toys. Should I start calling you Q?"

"Get serious, Sutherlin." His tone sharpens. "That flippant attitude is going to get you into trouble one day."

"Already did," I say dryly. "You suspended me, remember?"

"Yep. And that turned out for the best. You're where you need to be—home with your father. You're also in the middle of something big." His gaze holds mine. "I'm hearing noise, Sutherlin. Loud noise. No clear details yet—but something's coming to a head in Tidewell."

The gravity in his tone trips my internal warning system. "You mean something new?"

He nods once. "I'm afraid so. As soon as I hear more, I'll pass it along."

"Fair enough." We stand at the same time. "Let's go look at your gear."

We walk together to his unit in the parking lot. He pops his trunk, and I peer inside.

In addition to the drone, he gives me a burner phone. "Unregistered. No GPS. Use it sparingly."

I turn the slim phone over in my hand. "You're spoiling me," I say, only half joking.

"This will spoil you." He reaches back in and pulls out a palm-sized black monocular. "That's a thermal monocular. Picks up heat signatures. Works day or night. Used to be military only. Now anyone with a badge and a budget can get one."

My pulse kicks up a notch. "That could come in handy."

"And last but not least." He hands me a slim black device. "This is a signal scanner. If there's anything transmitting nearby—cameras, hidden routers—you'll know."

"This just went from recon to spy craft," I say.

His gaze hardens. "Because your local corruption just went to something bigger. Be careful, Sutherlin. Go on your stakeout, but if you stumble upon their trafficking operation, don't you dare go in alone. They won't hesitate to take you out."

The weight of my mission settles heavy in my bones. "Neither will I."

"I'm serious, Sutherlin. Promise me you won't go in alone."

I salute him. "I promise."

We transport the gear to my Bronco, and I slam the rear door shut. "I need another favor, Sarge. Will you see what you can dig up on The Overlook—permits, utilities, zoning flags? Look for anything that doesn't fit."

"I'm on it," he says. "I should have preliminary answers before you get back to Tidewell."

"Thank you, Sarge. I appreciate the support."

"Any time, Sutherlin. Just watch your back," he says, squeezing my shoulder.

"I hear you," I say quietly. "I can't afford to screw this up. Caroline's counting on me to find her embryos."

He opens my car door, and I slide behind the wheel. As I drive away, I glimpse Morales in the rearview mirror, standing in the parking lot watching me, concern etching his face.

I'm leaving the Richmond city limits when my phone lights up with Briggs's name. My heart skips a beat. I haven't heard from him since our argument in front of the Salty Bean Café yesterday.

I send it straight to voicemail. The clock is ticking, and I need to stay focused. He calls again. And again. Finally, on the fifth ring, I answer. "What do you want, Briggs?"

"To save your life. On second thought, maybe I should let the Old Guard deal with you."

I tighten my grip on the steering wheel. "Cut the crap, Briggs. What's the life-threatening emergency?"

"Travis Keene's body washed up at the marina boat ramp this morning. I just left the scene. The ME's preliminary examination reveals a blow to his head with a blunt-force object—consistent with the butt of a nine-millimeter Glock."

The bottom drops out of my gut. A nine-millimeter Glock, like the one holstered to my hip.

"This is serious, Lane. They're going to pin Keene's murder on you. They're not waiting for an official autopsy. They want you off the streets. Out of their shady business. They're planning to send a unit for you this afternoon as soon as Tate approves the arrest warrant."

I open my mouth to speak, but my tongue is tied. I've often wondered what it would feel like to be wrongly accused of a serious crime. Now I know. There are no words.

"Let me help you, Lane."

"Thanks. But I've got this. I appreciate the heads-up," I say, ending the call.

I step on the gas, my mind racing, my heart kicking into high gear. If they lock me up, they'll try to suicide me like they did Ben. I'll be defenseless behind bars.

They've backed me against the wall.

There's only one option left.

Run.

Chapter Twenty-Two

My thoughts scatter as I speed down the highway, the tires humming beneath me. Someone hit Travis Keene over the head with the pistol grip of a Glock after I left him on Wednesday night. And now Boone is gearing up to arrest me for murder.

They don't just want me silenced. They want me contained. In jail. Right where they can reach me. Where accidents happen.

I can run, but I can't go far. Not with Caroline's embryos still missing. Not with my name about to be dragged through the mud.

Two missions now—find the embryos and clear my name.

I consider my options. A hotel is out. The identification and credit card required would provide a neat little paper trail, gift wrapped for Boone. Camping's not happening without gear—my pup tent disintegrated sometime during the flip-phone era.

I need somewhere off the radar. Close enough to Tidewell to get back fast in an emergency but far enough to avoid Boone.

I call Caroline. She answers right away, as though she's been staring at her phone, willing it to ring. "Did you find my embryos?"

"Not yet. But I'm working a couple of new leads. If you're

inside the house, step outside for a minute. I don't want anyone overhearing this conversation."

"Sure. Hang on." Footsteps on hardwood are followed by the soft click of a door opening and closing. She's back on the line, her voice tight with worry. "What's wrong, Lane?"

"The local sheriff is planning to arrest me this afternoon for a crime I didn't commit."

"Oh, no! Is it related to the egg trafficking?"

"Not directly. But it's all connected—the same crime syndicate. I can't afford to get arrested. I'm no good to you in jail." I don't tell her what would really happen to me. There's no point in scaring her. "I need somewhere to stay. I was thinking—"

"Our house on the Corrotoman is perfect," Caroline blurts. "And I'm coming with you."

"Absolutely not, Caroline. These people mean business. You're much safer at River Birch. I'll ask Judd and Brandy to move into the house with you and Dad while I'm gone."

"Please, Lane, let me come with you. I can't just sit here and wait. I'm losing my mind."

The desperation in her tone tugs at my heartstrings. Besides, I enjoy her company, and she knows her family's property. "All right. But if you come with me, you do exactly as I say."

"I promise," she says, her tone now upbeat.

"Listen carefully. This is important. I'm twenty minutes away, and you need to be ready to leave when I get there. I won't have time to come inside. Pack a bag for me—toiletries and a few changes of clothes. Just throw things in. It doesn't matter what. There's a duffel bag and a backpack under the bed. I need those. Have everything waiting at the front door." I think about the mountain of luggage she brought with her. "And, Caroline, you're only allowed one bag."

She hesitates for a split second. "No problem. I'll pack lightly."

"Grab one of Dad's old-man hats and his trench coat from the front-hall closet. His car key should be in the dish on the table beside the door."

"Got it. But why do we need those things?"

"To ditch my shadow. He'll be on the lookout for me, not an old man in a Volvo wagon. Leave your phone at the house, but you can bring your laptop. Mine too. It's in my room. We'll keep them powered down unless we need them."

"Understood." She inhales a loud breath. "Let me get busy. Call if you think of something else."

The line goes dead before I can say goodbye. I place the dreaded call to my brother. When he answers, I can tell he's already wound tight. "I was getting ready to call you. I just got off the phone with Brody Talcott. The whole sheriff's department is out for blood, Lane. Yours."

My skin prickles. I already know this. But hearing it from my brother takes on new meaning. "I heard."

"You need to get the hell out of town. And fast. Judge Tate is in court until two. Once he approves the arrest warrant, they're coming for you."

I glance at the dashboard clock. That gives me an hour—more time than I thought.

"I have a plan, but it's safer if you don't know the details. Caroline's coming with me. We'll take Dad's car to throw off my tail. That should at least give me a head start."

"Smart thinking. I need to finish up some work, but I can head home soon. I want to be there when the deputies arrive. I hope Boone sends Clay. I can't wait to see his face when I tell him you skipped town."

"Be careful, Judd. Don't piss them off." I slow to a stop at a red light, drumming my fingers on the steering wheel. "Do you mind moving into the house while I'm gone? Dad shouldn't be alone at night."

"No problem," he says. "I already thought of that."

"What should we tell Lally and Shawna? I'm not sure how we explain my sudden disappearance. The less they know, the better."

"Leave that to me. I'll think of something." There's a pause on the line. When he speaks again, his voice is softer. "Laney, this isn't about pride or proving anything. If things go sideways, you don't push through. You disappear. You hear me?"

I close my eyes. "I hear you."

"Good. Because I can live with you running. I can't live with you dead."

I grip the wheel tighter. "I'll be careful."

"No," he says. "Be smart. Careful gets people killed."

I've barely hung up when Morales calls with the promised preliminary report on The Overlook.

"I've got the goods," he says. "Public records show Colt Craddock applied for an excavation and building permit three years ago to construct a wine cellar beneath an auxiliary building at The Overlook. The work was approved with minimal oversight. Utility records show electricity usage at the property increased nearly tenfold over the previous year—far beyond what's required for wine storage. Either that's one hell of a wine cellar, or he's operating something else down there—something that would require commercial or medical permits he never applied for."

"This all tracks. What else?"

"I received confirmation that Ellison and Colt knew each other at Duke. They weren't just friends. They were once romantically involved."

"That explains a lot." I check the clock. "I'm out of time, Sarge. I'll do recon in the morning. If anything looks suspicious, I'm going in."

"Not without me." There's a pause on the other end. "You don't sound right, Sutherlin. What's going on?"

"Boone has sent out a posse for me on trumped-up murder charges." I briefly tell him about Travis Keene and his relationship to Clay's trial.

"Listen to me, Sutherlin. You are not going in there alone. I repeat—do not make a move. We'll coordinate a time and place to meet in the morning."

"Ten-four," I say, half meaning it. Waiting may not be an option.

As predicted, Shadow Man's black Chevy is parked a hundred yards north of the farm entrance. I wiggle my fingers at him as I pass.

A fierce calm settles over me as I drive beneath the canopy of river birch trees, their branches arching overhead like a tunnel. Everything that matters is right here—on this farm. Whatever's coming, I won't let it touch my family.

Caroline is waiting at the front door when I pull into the circle. I kill the engine, power off my phone, and drop it in the cupholder. She hurries out with an armload of luggage, her head down, moving fast. I grab the gear Morales gave me, and together, we load everything into the back of Dad's wagon.

I pull a short gray wig from the duffel bag of disguises she retrieved from under my bed, stuff my ponytail beneath it, settle Dad's hat on top, and shrug into his trench coat. Not perfect, but from a distance, I look enough like an old man to fool Shadow Man.

"Get in the back seat and lie down," I order her, cringing at the edge in my voice.

When he was still driving, Dad used to keep an old blanket in the back—something to throw over his legs on cold mornings out on the water in his boat. The faint smell of salt and diesel drifts up as I spread it over her. "Sorry about the odor. We'll be out of town soon, and you can take it off."

I slide behind the wheel and drive out to the road. I pass Shadow Man without looking his way, my eyes fixed on the ribbon of asphalt ahead of me. I don't breathe again until the rearview mirror shows nothing but empty pavement.

I take the long way out of town, skirting downtown and the sheriff's department entirely.

Once we're safely on the highway, Caroline climbs into the front seat and buckles her seatbelt. She exhales—long and shaky—like she's been holding her breath since I called. "I feel like I've stumbled into a spy movie. What crime are they framing you for?"

"Murder."

I tell her about Addie's death, Clay's trial, and the tampered jury. About Judge Tate. Sheriff Boone. The Night Ryders.

She slides her sunglasses down her nose to look at me. "Why do the Night Ryders need to keep order? Is there that much crime in Tidewell?"

"That's the irony. There's practically none. At least not from the citizens. The ones who should be arrested are wearing badges."

She shakes her head. "You've been through a lot these past couple of months. Then I show up with my baggage, dragging you deeper into this mess."

"Don't go there, Caroline. I was already investigating the egg trafficking. You just fast-tracked me."

As we cross the Rappahannock River Bridge into White Stone, I fill her in on everything I learned from Kincaid and Morales.

"Do you really think my embryos might be at Craddock estate?" she asks quietly.

I glance over at her. "I don't want you to get your hopes up. It's a long shot."

"And if they're not there?"

"Then they were moved—probably to a major northeastern city. I'll be honest, Caroline. Time is not on our side."

She nods, staring out the window, silent until we reach Kilmarnock.

"We'll need some groceries," she says finally. "Your choices are Food Lion or Walmart."

"Walmart. They sell ammo."

Chapter Twenty-Three

Caroline's family home—a new farmhouse built to feel settled and timeless—sits at the tip of a peninsula on fifty acres, the Corrotoman River wrapping around it on three sides, water stretching to the horizon in every direction. A gravel drive snakes a quarter mile from the two-lane country road, cutting through dense pine forest before opening onto the wide expanse of the house and freshly plowed fields.

The setting is serene. Remote. And if things go wrong, it's nearly impossible to reach without being seen.

The living space is one open room—kitchen flowing into dining, anchored by a massive stone fireplace in the family room. In a glass-walled corner, part sunroom, part conservatory, a Steinway baby grand waits.

Caroline deposits her belongings in the private suite occupying one wing of the first floor, then leads me upstairs to a spacious guest room with an ensuite bath and balcony overlooking the river.

We bundle up in hats and scarves and walk down to the water to catch the last of the daylight. Sandy beaches soften the riprapped shoreline, and from the end of the long dock, we can see the mouth of the Rappahannock River. The setting sun reflects off the glassy water in bands of gold, stealing my breath.

Based on my knowledge of local geography, it would take thirty minutes to reach The Overlook by boat. The idea tugs at me—tempting. But even if I had access to one, I'm better off on land, with the surrounding woods to provide cover.

The temperature drops as we return to the house. Caroline heads to the kitchen to work on dinner while I start a fire in the living room.

I stack kindling in the fireplace and strike a match. The fire catches quickly, flames licking up the stone, warming the room and softening the edges of the day. For the first time since Briggs warned me about my impending arrest, my world feels almost still.

I pour myself a glass of wine and watch Caroline move easily around the kitchen as she throws together a homemade pizza and tossed salad.

"This place suits you, Caroline. Do you spend much time here?"

She smiles as she slides the pizza into the oven. "I love it here. So did Julian. This is the one place he could truly relax—away from the demands of his career." Her voice softens. "It was meant to be my parents' retirement home. But Mom was diagnosed with Alzheimer's while the house was still under construction. Dad hardly ever comes here now. I think the ghosts of what might have been haunt him." She hesitates. "Maybe if he had grandchildren . . ."

She closes the oven door, and when she turns back toward me, her eyes are shiny with unshed tears. "You told me in the car not to get my hopes up. But it's hard not to when there's nothing else to hope for."

"It may feel that way now, but you still have your music," I say gently. "And you're young. You could find love again."

She shakes her head. "Julian and I had something rare—the

kind of love you only find once." Her voice drops. "Besides . . . I have no eggs left. This is my only chance to have children."

"There's always adoption," I say, but the words sound thin even to my own ears.

"Adoption is a great option for some. Just not for me." She swipes at her eyes. "I didn't mean to get sappy on you. I'm still processing my grief—and with the hormone prep for the embryo transfer, my emotions are all over the place."

I nod, letting the words settle. There's nothing to fix, nothing to say that won't feel like trespassing. Some losses need space, not answers.

After we clean up from dinner, we sit by the fire, the wine warming us as the flames crackle low and steady.

"What about you, Lane?" she asks softly. "Is there a special someone in your life?"

Briggs flickers through my mind, but I push him aside. "I'm still recovering from my divorce."

"Divorce?" Her brow lifts. "I didn't know. You're so young."

"We were married three years. Long enough for him to cheat."

She grimaces. "I'm sorry. Some men are such jerks."

I laugh, but it fades quickly. Briggs creeps back into my thoughts, and I glance down, picking at a loose thread on the sofa. "There's . . . someone. I thought we had a connection. But we're too much alike. Both stubborn. Both driven."

And suddenly it clicks—why Alex unsettles me. She isn't the problem. She just wears the same shape as the past. The woman my husband had an affair with. The one who shattered everything I thought was solid.

Once burned, twice shy. I'm not sure I'll ever trust a man again.

I vowed not to think about Briggs while the investigation is underway. But the truth is, there will always be another case. Another crisis. This is who I am. I chase criminals and keep people safe. At least I try. Some people are their own worst enemies.

Caroline has fallen asleep on the sofa, her glass tilted dangerously in her hand. I smile at her—at how easily she's slipped into my life. I've helped all kinds of women—the homeless, the addicted, the abused. But I've never let myself get close to one like this before. I'm fully invested in finding her embryos. She's a good person who deserves a future.

I slip the glass from her hand and gently shake her. "Come on, sleepyhead. Time for bed. I'll close up down here."

She stirs, mumbling the alarm code as she shuffles toward the stairs.

When the fire burns down to embers, I check the doors and windows and set the alarm. I don't expect trouble out here in the middle of nowhere, but caution is a habit I can't afford to break.

Upstairs, I slip between absurdly high-thread-count sheets and pull the duvet over me. The house feels solid—thick walls, tall ceilings, state-of-the-art systems. Safe.

And yet sleep won't come.

My mind circles my family—Judd, Brandy, Dad. Worst-case scenarios crowd the dark. I put them in danger, then walked away. What if the Craddocks recognized Dad as the old man they jerked around in the boathouse? What if the Night Ryders decide to make an example of him? Or Judd? He's a lifetime hunter, an excellent shot, but will he pull the trigger if someone threatens his life? To protect his wife? Their unborn child?

I bolt upright, heart hammering. Clearing my name of Travis Keene's murder charges will be difficult with Tate and Boone running this town. But I can't let this drag on. I can't keep my family in the crosshairs.

Maybe once I find Caroline's embryos, I'll turn myself in. If I'm behind bars, at least they won't need to come after the people I love.

Chapter Twenty-Four

Caroline sleeps in on Saturday morning. I tiptoe around, making coffee and straightening the kitchen, careful not to wake her.

I haven't heard from Morales about a meeting time or place. While I'd prefer to have a partner for this mission, I can't afford to wait.

I head outside to Dad's Volvo, where, among the other gear Morales gave me, I find a handheld police scanner. I set it on the console, power it up, and keep the volume low as I finish loading my backpack. I throw in a dark hoodie and a paper map from Dad's glove box—creased, outdated, but reliable.

Leaning against the front of the car, I power up the burner phone and punch in Judd's number.

"Hello?" He sounds sleepy. Guarded.

"Judd, it's me. I'm calling from a burner phone. Don't save it as a contact, but now you've got a number if you need to reach me."

"Got it," he says, instantly sharper. "Are you okay?"

"For now. You?"

"All good," he says. "The house is quiet this morning. But you missed the spectacle yesterday. Boone had the nerve to send Clay to arrest you. Dad was in rare form—Judge Sutherlin at his finest. When they insisted on searching the house, he followed them around, poking his cane at them when they touched something, rattling off a long list of charges he would throw at them if they didn't get off his property."

I laugh despite the seriousness of the situation. "I shouldn't laugh, but that's funny."

"And get this. Dad questioned him about Addie's death. He all but called Clay a murderer to his face."

I smile to myself. "It helps to know the real dad is still in there somewhere."

"He was vintage Dad. I wish you had been here." A pause. "But Lane, there's more. Things in town are getting stranger by the minute."

I brace myself. "Stranger, how?"

"There was a party at Slip 99 last night. Nothing wild—an impromptu get-together of locals who wanted to blow off steam."

I grip the phone tighter. I already know where this is going. "And?"

"The Night Ryders rolled in around nine and shut it down. Ran everyone off. Hauled in a few folks for show." He exhales. "Cooter was pissed. And I don't blame him. He's got a business to run."

"Was anyone hurt?"

"Not badly. But the message was clear. This isn't about keeping the peace anymore. They want to own us."

Anger surges through me. "I've had enough of the Night Ryders. They don't get to tell us where and when we gather." I push off the fender. "Keep your head down, Judd. Stay put at the farm. I won't be gone much longer."

"Be careful, Lane."

I end the call and power off the phone.

I glance around, half expecting to see a long line of Night Ryder trucks barreling down the driveway. What happens if we don't stop them? Cooter—and a whole lot of others—will go out of business. I refuse to let my town fold.

I can't wait any longer. Morales or not, I'm moving forward.

I head back inside, where I find Caroline in the kitchen. "Good morning! Time for fun and games."

I don't need to tell her where I'm going. We discussed the stakeout at length over dinner.

I grab a banana out of the fruit bowl. "I'm going to take a quick shower. I'll be down in a minute."

She nods. "I'll have a fresh cup of coffee waiting for you."

I shower and dress in warm, dark clothes. When I return to the kitchen, she hands me a coffee in a to-go cup. "Are you coming back?" she asks, her eyes searching mine.

"I'm counting on it. If something happens and I'm unavoidably detained, I'll get word to you. Probably by email."

"Good. I'll check it often," she says, a tremor beneath her calm.

I take her by the shoulders. "Listen to me, Caroline. I have to do this. Not just for you but for all the other women who've been robbed. No matter what happens today, you're going to be okay. You'll move forward. Julian would want that."

She blinks, fighting tears.

"You have your music," I add softly. "It's more than a gift. It's how you survive. Hold on to that."

I hand her a slip of paper with Morales's phone number and email address. "If something goes wrong, contact Sergeant Joe Morales at Richmond PD. Call him if you can get to a phone."

"I'm regretting talking Dad out of installing a landline."

I laugh. "Landlines are only good in situations like these. And hopefully you're never in a situation like this again. Email him—he'll respond right away. Memorize the information. Then get rid of it."

Caroline looks at the slip of paper, then back at me. "Got it."

She walks me to the door. "Be careful, Lane. I'll have dinner ready when you get back."

Guilt grips my chest as I pull away in Dad's wagon. I

shouldn't be leaving her here without a car. Without a phone. I remind myself that this is her family's house. She has her laptop. Neighbors aren't close, but they exist. If she has to walk, she can.

I draw a steadying breath. I'll do everything in my power to be back for dinner.

I wait until I'm on the main road before calling Morales from the burner phone. He answers right away, and I blurt, "I'm on my way to The Overlook."

"Sutherlin!" he roars. "I specifically instructed you to wait."

"I realize that. And I'm specifically disobeying that instruction. I'm a consultant, not a full-time detective on your staff. Instead of arguing, let's talk strategy. I need backup. We can't trust Boone's deputies."

He exhales a resigned breath. "Sutherlin, you give me more gray hairs than my own kids." A pause. "As for backup, I'm one step ahead of you. State police are moving units into the area. They're staging now—quietly."

"Good. Then let's not disappoint them."

"We don't have a warrant," he says in a sharp tone. "I need eyes first, Lane. Drone footage. Phone video. Any kind of legitimate proof."

"And if they're already moving evidence?"

"Then we don't wait. Keep the burner phone on. Stay in touch. I'm leaving Richmond now, but I'm ninety minutes away. I've got your six, Sutherlin," he says, ending the call.

I stop at a convenience store just outside of White Stone. I purchase a bottled water, more black coffee, and a protein bar. I don't linger. I don't make eye contact. I'm in and out in less than five.

Twenty minutes later, I ease Dad's wagon down a narrow service road and park beneath a stand of pines a quarter mile from The Overlook. I finish the approach on foot, keeping the trees between me and the property. The land rises here, giving way to a broad clearing below. At this distance, the estate looks almost peaceful—a red brick Georgian house set high above the river, manicured lawns sloping toward the water, the outbuilding tucked discreetly near the tree line.

Crouching behind a fallen oak, I unzip my pack, pulling out the drone and its controller, which has its own built-in screen. I power it on, and the rotors whisper to life, barely audible as I send it climbing. The live feed sharpens, and suddenly I'm hovering above the property, seeing what no one is meant to see.

The Overlook is larger than it appears from the road. The main house dominates the rise, symmetrical and stately, all white trim and shuttered windows. But my focus slides past it to the auxiliary building, which I once mistook for a barn.

From above, the structure is long and low, its roofline recently repaired, the surrounding ground scraped clean. Tire tracks cut deep into the dirt behind it. Power lines snake toward it, far too many for storage or livestock.

Movement flickers at the edges of the frame. I guide the drone lower. Two SUVs and a boxy cargo truck bearing the *MidAtlantic BioLogistics* logo are parked behind the building. Men stand watch, spaced out around the perimeter, cradling weapons like they're waiting to use them.

This isn't casual. They mean business.

The building's doors slide open—not swinging doors but mechanized ones, rolling smoothly upward. Behind them waits another set. Industrial. Steel. Reinforced. The kind you don't install unless you're sealing something in.

They retract with mechanical precision, revealing the empty back bed of a cargo truck. Bright lights flood the space, stark and unforgiving.

My stomach knots.

Figures emerge from inside the building. Women. At least a dozen—maybe more. They move slowly, guarded on either side, hands resting instinctively on rounded bellies.

Pregnant.

Some far along. Others not yet showing much, but enough that there's no mistaking what I'm seeing.

The guards usher the women into the truck, one by one. There's no resistance—just resignation. One guard stands at the door with a clipboard, checking them off as they disappear inside. The drone camera wobbles as my grip tightens around the controller. The truck door slams shut. The vehicle backs out, circling wide around the clearing before heading toward the waterfront.

I'm on my feet and moving through the woods as the drone tracks the truck down to the dock. A cargo boat idles at the end—steel-hulled, broad-beamed, utilitarian. No markings. Built to carry weight. Not passengers.

The truck is backing toward the open hold when the shouting starts. My pulse spikes. They've spotted the drone. Voices rise—sharp, urgent—as men fan out with weapons drawn, sweeping the perimeter with practiced precision.

The drone picks up more movement back near the auxiliary building. Colt steps into view, phone pressed to his ear, eyes cutting straight toward the woods. Toward me.

I fumble for the burner phone and punch Morales's number.

He answers immediately. "Talk to me, Sutherlin."

"They're on the move," I whisper. "They're transporting pregnant women in a truck to Craddock's dock. A cargo boat is waiting. This is human trafficking, Morales. Women being trafficked for pregnancy. "

Silence. Then his voice hardens. "You need to get out. State police are moving in. They'll take over."

"Too late. Colt already knows someone's onto him." Branches snap to my left. "I hear them. They're looking for me, heading toward me."

"Then listen to me carefully—"

A figure breaks from the trees. Colt Craddock—polished and calm. He's holding a pistol—long-barreled, old, the kind of weapon collectors covet. He doesn't shout, doesn't hesitate. He raises his weapon and fires once high, deliberate. A warning.

I bolt.

Everything happens at once—boots pounding behind me, men shouting orders. I ditch the drone and run blindly through the woods. Branches whip my face. Roots grab at my feet. I veer hard left, then right, trying to break their line of sight.

Another shot cracks the air. Not close enough to hit. Close enough to warn.

I skid to a stop behind a stand of scrub pines, doubled over, chest heaving.

Colt emerges from the trees ten yards ahead of me. He actually appears amused. Every hair on his perfectly styled head is in place, his waxed jacket pristine—untouched by dirt or sweat—like he hasn't moved an inch while the rest of his men scramble. The long-barreled pistol rests easily in his hand, pointed at the ground. Not threatening. Yet.

"You're persistent," he says mildly. "I'll give you that."

I don't raise my hands. I don't reach for my weapon. I hold his gaze, steady and unflinching. "You're done, Colt. This is over."

He smiles—a slow, knowing curve of his mouth. "Wrong. I'm only getting started."

"*Wrong*. Your daddy is dead. There's no one left to clean up after you. Judge Tate can't save you now."

His smile sharpens. "You really have no idea what you stumbled into."

He lifts his pistol, leveling it at my chest.

Strangely, I'm not afraid. This ends now—one way or another.

Another siren cuts through the woods, closer now. Colt's eyes flick past me, calculating. Then the woods explode with sound.

"*State police! Drop the weapon!*"

Blue lights strobe through the trees. Troopers pour in from every direction—weapons trained, voices commanding. A helicopter dips low overhead, spotlight blazing.

Colt exhales once, long and controlled, and lowers the gun.

They take him down hard. Efficient. Relentless. No ceremony.

As they haul him past me, cuffs biting into his wrists, he meets my eyes.

"This is war, Detective," he says quietly. "And wars don't end when one man falls."

I stand frozen as Morales pushes through the line of troopers and grips my arm.

"You okay?" he demands.

I nod, adrenaline still roaring. "Yeah."

He looks past me—to the dock, the auxiliary building, the chaos unfolding. "You did good, Lane."

The arrests will make headlines. But the war Colt promised is already moving—quiet, hidden, and aimed straight at the people I love.

Chapter Twenty-Five

I've walked into crime scenes that still smelled of blood and smoke and death.

This is much worse.

The auxiliary building has been hollowed out and rebuilt into something sleek and efficient—garages and offices on the ground level, a legitimate face for an illegitimate operation. But underground, where no one was meant to look, are laboratories, cryogenic tanks, and sterile rooms designed for one purpose only.

To turn stolen eggs into babies.

And the women who carried them? They weren't volunteers. They were assets. Also stolen.

I spend hours talking to them, listening to their stories—at least the ones who speak English. They come from all over the world, snatched from their lives and transported here to be surrogate mothers. Some were promised work. Some were coerced. Others were simply taken.

This web is so intricate, I don't know how to begin untangling it.

I ask some of the women about the people who abducted them. They describe a large man with dark, curly hair and mean eyes. When I show them a photo of Milo pulled from the internet, they don't identify him as the one who kidnapped them—but as the man who delivered them here.

I write down names and numbers and begin calling families, letting them know their daughters are alive, safe for now, and will be in touch soon. It's a logistical nightmare. Some of the women are due to deliver any day. Others are only weeks along.

None of them know anything about the women whose children they're carrying. Those children belong to women who never consented to become mothers—not yet, not like this. Eggs harvested. Embryos implanted. Lives set in motion without permission. The biological mothers must be identified. Notified. Given the right to decide what comes next.

I can't let myself think about the men who donated the sperm, or the fallout that's coming—the marriages that will fracture, the lives that will implode—when the truth finally surfaces.

When I'm able to break away, I head straight to the main cryogenic storage room. The tanks hum softly, steady and impersonal, stainless-steel cylinders arranged in neat rows. Each one is labeled. Coded. Logged. More inventory.

I scan the manifests until my vision blurs, searching for Caroline's name, for any reference to her embryos. Some tanks hold eggs. Other embryos are already fertilized and frozen, their futures suspended in liquid nitrogen.

This part, at least, appears intact. Monitored. Maintained. Whoever built this operation understood the science. These embryos were meant to survive. Caroline's may be here. Or they may already be gone—implanted without her knowledge, her body replaced by another woman's whose consent was never given.

I pull aside the crime scene tech who's running point and give her Caroline Edwards's name, spelling it twice.

"If you come across anything tied to her—labels, manifests, storage logs—I need to know."

She exhales. "That's like finding a needle in a haystack."

"I realize that. But her husband died a few months ago. Those embryos are all she has left."

Something shifts in her expression. "I'll flag the name and make sure it gets passed to the lab team. If it's here, we'll find it."

I smile at her. "Thank you."

Turning away, I spot Morales wandering around the lab, seemingly overwhelmed by the scale of the operation.

"It's staggering, isn't it?" I say.

"It'll take weeks—maybe months—to untangle the records," he says. "A Richmond fertility clinic has already agreed to oversee the tanks under court order. The embryos and eggs will be safe under the watchful eyes of their trained staff."

I nod. "That's good news. What do I tell Caroline Edwards?"

Morales studies me for a long moment. "Tell her we're doing everything by the book."

I let out a low whistle. "That won't be easy. She's already on pins and needles. Even waiting another day will be torture." I look past him at the traffic in the hallway. "What's going on outside?"

"Federal agents are handing out charges at a steady clip—trafficking, kidnapping, conspiracy, fraud, weapons violations."

My gaze shifts back to Morales. "Any sign of Milo?"

His expression hardens. "He wouldn't be stupid enough to show his face here."

"Do you know where he is?" I press. "Have you spoken to him today?"

"It's Saturday, Lane. He's probably home watching football."

"Some of the pregnant women identified him as the man who brought him here." I hold his gaze. "He's guilty, Sarge. The sooner you accept that, the better for all of us."

He shoots me a warning look. "Let me worry about Milo. The press has arrived in force. You should handle the press conference. It's a big deal, and you've earned it."

I don't hesitate. "Yes, sir. I just need a minute to freshen up. I'll meet you out front."

We split up outside the lab. I find the ladies' room and splash cold water on my face, trying to steady my breath. I'm blotting my skin with a brown paper towel when a familiar reflection appears in the mirror behind me.

Wylie Craddock.

"What do you want?" I say, crumbling the towel and tossing it in the trash.

His eyes bore into mine through the mirror. "To thank you. You did me a favor by getting rid of my brother for me. Now that he'll be spending the foreseeable future in prison, I'll be moving into The Overlook." He hunches his shoulders. "Someone has to look after the estate."

I spin around to face him. "About that. I'm curious why your parents left The Overlook to him and not both of you."

A muscle in his jaw twitches.

"Oops. Did I strike a nerve?"

His mouth curves into something close to a smile. "You, of all people, should know how parents like to play favorites. Especially fathers. Tommy was the favorite in yours, wasn't he, Laney?"

His comment cuts deep. But I don't give him the satisfaction of letting it show.

"What part did you play in your brother's trafficking scheme?" I ask coolly. "If Milo was the Reaper, what does that make you and Colt—the overseers?"

He laughs—sharp, unhinged—the sound making my stomach drop. "I see you've done your homework. You're correct. Milo was the Reaper—the fixer, the one who cleans up the messes."

His smile thins. "But Colt? Colt was the Broker. The arranger. He matched egg to buyer. Managed supply and demand."

He leans closer, voice lowering. "But this was all Colt's operation. You won't find a single shred of evidence tying it to me."

"Funny. Men who say that usually know where the bodies are buried."

"You're a nuisance, Sutherlin." His lip curls. "I could wrap my hands around your neck and choke the life out of you—"

I don't wait for him to finish that thought. I drive the edge of my hand into his throat—hard, precise. A textbook strike. His eyes bulge as the air leaves him in a strangled gasp. I follow with a sharp sweep to his legs, sending him crashing to the tile.

He hits the floor coughing, clawing for breath.

I plant my foot beside his head and look down at him, calm as glass.

"Don't ever threaten me again," I say quietly.

I straighten my jacket and smooth my ponytail before heading outside to face the press. A makeshift podium has been set up, the auxiliary building looming behind it.

The local FBI special agent in charge steps forward, offers brief remarks, then introduces me.

I keep my statement short.

"Our investigation into Dr. Margaret Ellison's death and the fire at the Willow Creek Fertility Clinic led us to significant irregularities involving harvested eggs and fertilized embryos. Those leads brought us here—to The Overlook. Colt Craddock, the owner of this estate, is the central figure in the egg trafficking operation. I have reason to believe he is part a of larger crime syndicate exerting control over the town of Tidewell."

The questions come fast and loud. I answer what I can, deflect what I must. Active investigation. Ongoing. Multiple arrests. No further comment.

"Detective Sutherlin—"

I recognize the voice before I find the face. Alex.

"Is it true you're wanted on murder charges in Tidewell?"

A murmur ripples through the crowd.

I meet her gaze, steady. "Yes. An arrest warrant has been issued."

Cameras zoom in.

I release a slow breath. "Here's the context. Travis Keene—the man whose death I'm accused of—served on the jury that acquitted Clay Dalton in his wife's murder trial. Mr. Keene contacted me, requesting a meeting on the night he died. He knew

I was informally investigating the possibility of jury tampering, and he had evidence that Judge Vernon Tate coerced the jury, leading to the acquittal. Mr. Keene told me he was being threatened. He feared for his life. Only minutes after I left him, Mr. Keene was attacked."

I let the words settle.

"Someone documented my departure with a set of photos. Before an autopsy was even conducted, an arrest warrant was sought for me."

Alex presses. "Why are you willing to comment on the Keene murder investigation but not on the reproductive trafficking uncovered here?"

Reproductive trafficking. That's not a term I've heard before. But how fitting. And chilling. It implies a broader spectrum of exploitation—women reduced to vessels, babies reduced to commodities.

I gesture to the auxiliary building behind me. "There are innocent victims in this case, Alex, and they deserve protection—not speculation."

I scan the crowd, slowly and deliberately. "As for the syndicate behind these crimes, sunlight is the best disinfectant. I didn't kill Travis Keene. And if I'm taken into custody by Sheriff Boone before this investigation is resolved, I fear I won't survive to tell the truth."

Silence falls heavy.

Before I even step away from the podium, I already know this won't stay local.

The questions are sharper. The cameras bigger. The attention relentless.

Tidewell has just gone national.

Chapter Twenty-Six

I turn the press conference over to Morales and slip away unnoticed. After retrieving the drone, I hurry back to my car and head in the opposite direction of Tidewell, driving until I'm sure no one is following me.

Night has fallen, and the country road stretches ahead of me—dark and uncertain. I can either continue on to Caroline's house, or I can make a U-turn back toward River Birch. I hate to leave Caroline stranded without a car.

But I need to check in with my family—to be with them if and when the fallout from the press conference rains down. And I need to get my phone out of my Bronco. It's been days. There's no telling what messages await me.

Boone won't take the press conference lying down. I can already picture him, face beaming red with fury. He won't back down. He'll be more determined than ever to get rid of me.

Then there's Wylie Craddock. Taking him down in the restroom felt damn good, but he'll be out for blood now too. Wylie Craddock doesn't lose. He just waits.

Bring it on, cowboy. That's what you get for threatening me.

A crackling noise reminds me the police scanner is still on in my pocket. I place it on the dashboard and listen as the dispatcher barks out orders regarding an incident in historic Captain's Row.

My stomach drops. That's where Lally lives.

I turn up the volume. All law enforcement and fire units have been dispatched to a house fire on Pelican's Way.

Lally lives on Pelican's Way.

I make a sharp left turn at the next intersection and circle back toward town.

My heart sinks when my burner phone lights up with a call from Judd. This can't be good. He would only call this number in an emergency.

He delivers the news I'm dreading. "Lally's house is on fire."

"I heard about it on the police scanner. Are you sure it's *her* house?"

"I'm positive. A friend of mine lives in that neighborhood. He knows Lally works for us. He called me."

"Do they know how the fire started?"

"Someone threw a Molotov cocktail through her living room window. The vehicle matched the description of Colter Craddock's black pickup. An eyewitness confirmed the vanity plate—OUTLAW."

Anger flashes through me. "They're retaliating against me. And they're not even trying to hide it."

"You messed with the wrong people, and now they're coming after the people you care about. Lally's first. Then comes Dad, Brandy, and me. Nobody's safe."

Guilt knots my stomach. "I'm so sorry, Judd."

"I'm sorry too, Lane. But this isn't on you. You're doing your job. This is on them—the Craddocks. And it has to stop."

"Are any of Lally's children still living with her?"

"No. But her oldest, John Henry, lives nearby. I just talked to her. She was so hysterical she couldn't get her words out. She handed the phone to John Henry. According to him, the house is going down fast. It's ancient—dry as kindling. I hope you don't mind. I offered for her to stay with us as long as she needs."

Tears sting my eyes. "Of course. It's the least we can do after everything she's done for us. Poor Lally. She raised all her children there." I swipe at my face. "Thanks for calling me. I'm headed out to Captain's Row now. I'll be in touch."

I pull into the parking lot of a convenience store and put the wagon in park. Colter Craddock threw a Molotov cocktail through Lally's living room window. This is no longer a battle. This is war.

Why isn't Colter in custody? With his father arrested and the operation exposed, he should be the first person the state police bring in for questioning. Unless Boone's protecting him. Which means Colter knows exactly how much time he has before they come for him.

I log into my Gmail account and send Caroline a message.

Have you heard the news? Colt Craddock has been arrested, and state police are now in control of his operation. It's a logistical mess right now, but the lead crime-scene investigator promised to flag anything connected to you. Another Richmond fertility clinic will oversee the cryogenic tanks under court order. It may take a few days to sort things out and get some answers, but everything is being handled by the book.

Another urgent situation has pulled me back to Tidewell. I'm not sure when I'll be able to get away. If you don't feel safe alone, I can send Judd to get you.

Her reply pops up almost immediately.

I've been glued to the news all afternoon. You did an excellent job with the press conference. Thank you for keeping me updated.

Don't worry about me. I'm fine here alone. If you can't make it back, my dad will come for me. I've been emailing him. He knows where I am.

Be careful, Lane. I'm worried about you.

Caroline wouldn't tell me if she felt unsafe, but knowing she's in touch with her father steadies me a little.

I put the car in gear and head back toward Tidewell.

By the time I arrive, Captain's Row is sealed off, the streets choked with emergency vehicles and flashing lights. I park Dad's wagon several blocks away and slip into the crowd gathered behind the tape.

I spot Lally with her son. John Henry has an arm around her shoulders, holding her trembling body upright. In all the years I've known her, I've never once seen her cry—not even the night Tommy died. She's always been the pillar that held my family together. Now it's our turn to support her.

Her house is fully engulfed. Flames roar through the windows, devouring the interior, lighting exposed studs like a skeleton on fire. Smoke pours into the night sky, thick and acrid, carrying the sharp smell of burning wood and insulation.

A sob breaks loose before I can stop it. I take a step toward her—

A hand clamps over my mouth and jerks me backward.

"Are you out of your mind?" a voice murmurs at my ear. *Briggs.* "What the hell are you doing here?"

"That's Lally," I say, my lip quivering, tears burning hot behind my eyes. "That's her house."

"I know, Laney." He pulls me against him. "But it's not safe for you to be here."

"Let me go, Briggs." I push at his chest, but his grip tightens. "I need to talk to her. I need to tell her I'm sorry. This is my fault."

His hold doesn't waver. "Colter Craddock is counting on you running straight to Lally's side. He's watching. And waiting." His voice drops. "You're in grave danger."

The fight drains out of me as I sag against him. "You're right. I need to leave."

He loosens his grip but doesn't step away, his body angled protectively between me and the street. "You're coming home with me."

I start to argue—I need to get to River Birch. But I'm of no use to my family in the state I'm in. I need somewhere to land—if only long enough to pull myself together.

"Okay," I murmur. "But only for a minute."

He pulls off his baseball cap and settles it low over my head. "I'm parked a couple of blocks over."

"I need my car. I'll meet you there."

When I pull into his driveway ten minutes later, Briggs's Tahoe is already parked out front, but the house is dark. He opens the door before I can knock, pulling me inside and locking it behind us.

He cups my face, his touch gentle, grounding. "I'm so sorry, Lane. About our fight. About everything." His mouth brushes mine—soft and reverent. "Thank God you're okay. I've been sick with worry."

"I'm a big girl, Briggs," I whisper. "I can take care of myself."

"Yes. You can." His gaze holds mine, full of something fierce and steady. "You proved that today."

When he kisses me this time, I don't resist. We stumble backward into the living room, urgency threading through relief, hands finding familiar ground.

———

We end up on the sofa, the house still dark. Briggs leans back against the cushions, and I curl into his side, his arm settling around my shoulders like it knows where it belongs. Neither of us speaks. We don't need to.

The quiet doesn't hold.

The weight of the day presses back in, heavy and relentless. "Lally doesn't deserve this," I say finally. "She lost her house, and it's all my fault. How will I ever face her again?"

"Hey." He tilts my chin until I'm looking at him. "This wasn't your fault."

I shake my head. "You're wrong. They went after her because they couldn't get to me."

"We're all in this together—a battle of good versus evil. Everyone knows you're our warrior, the one leading the charge to save us. You're a local hero."

I grunt. "Since when?"

"Since always. Your family's been part of this town longer than most people can remember. Your father helped a lot of folks when he was on the bench. Judd's solid. Always has been." He hesitates, then adds, "And Tommy . . . nineteen years gone, but nobody's forgotten him."

I shift to face him. "What about Roxie?"

He lets out a soft chuckle. "Your mother's in a class all her own."

"A class of what?" I murmur.

"I'm not answering that." He closes his eyes, leaving one slightly cracked. "This changes things between us, you know."

I run my finger along his lips. "Really? How so?"

"You have to call me Lawson from now on."

I laugh, but he doesn't. He serious.

"*Lawson*," I say softly, testing the name. "I'll see what I can do."

I settle back into the crook of his arm. "About our fight. You weren't completely wrong. Just . . . not completely right either. I'm not threatened by other women. I'm just particular about the company I keep."

He kisses my hair. "I stand corrected."

I snuggle deeper into the sofa cushions. "I can't stop thinking about Lally. She was more of a mother to me than Roxie."

Briggs nods. "She was a second mother to us all. After football practice, she'd sit us down on the back steps and check us over, taking inventory of our bruises." He exhales. "And she never missed a home game. She was always in the front row, wearing that red hat with the white pom pom, cheering us on like we were her own."

For the first time today, my body stops bracing for the next blow. We trade a few more stories, the kind that don't need punchlines or endings. Outside, the house creaks softly as the night settles in. And I finally close my eyes.

169

I wake in Briggs's arms, his hand warm and steady around my waist. I close my eyes again, breathing him in, pretending the outside world doesn't exist. We fell asleep on the sofa, drifting off while trading Lally stories.

Then it all rushes back, like a storm surge crashing over a peaceful shoreline. The showdown at The Overlook. Wylie lying on the restroom floor. The press conference. Colt throwing a Molotov cocktail through Lally's window—her house burning to the ground.

A phone vibrates against my left hip. I pull it from between the sofa cushions and elbow Briggs. "Your phone's ringing."

He answers in a gruff, "Lawson Briggs."

Lawson. I promised to call him that last night after we . . .

I don't let my mind go there. Not yet.

I'm not sure I can call him Lawson. Tommy always called him Briggs, and switching now feels like betrayal—however ridiculous that sounds.

I'm close enough to hear the voice on the other end of the line. Male. About my age. I can't quite place it. He's asking to speak to me.

"She's not answering her phone," the man says. "I saw you together last night at the fire. Is she still with you?"

Briggs's jaw tightens. "Who is this?" he barks.

"I'd rather not say. Please. This is urgent." The desperation in his voice is so achingly familiar it hits me in the chest. *Ben.*

Briggs hands me the phone without a word. I roll off the sofa, taking the blanket with me, and move toward the window. Outside, the sun has just crested over Oyster Bay, the sky washed in pinks and golds—so beautiful and yet so wrong for a world that's coming apart.

"Lane," Ben says quietly. "I need to see you in person."

"What's this about? Are you in trouble?"

A pause. Long enough to set my nerves humming. "No. But you are. It's about Travis Keene. And Clay Dalton."

My grip tightens on the phone. "What about them?"

"We shouldn't talk about it over the phone. Can you meet me at the Tide House in twenty minutes?"

I glance back at Briggs, who has a sofa cushion spread across his bare lap. He's listening, even though he's pretending not to.

My eyes scan the room—clothes strewn everywhere. I must look a mess. "Give me thirty minutes."

"Fine," Ben says, and the line goes dead.

Tossing Briggs his phone, I gather up my clothes with one hand while holding the blanket tight around me with the other.

"Who was that?" Briggs calls after me as I head down the hall to the powder room.

"Business. I need to hurry. I'll tell you about it later."

I clean up as best I can—washing my face, tying my hair back, rinsing out my mouth. When I emerge, Briggs is waiting by the front door—chest bare, impressive abs, jeans slung low over his hips.

"We need to talk about last night," he says.

I study his face. Is that uncertainty? Or worse—regret? I can't do this. Not now. Not today.

"There's nothing to talk about," I say easily. "It was just a hookup. You don't owe me anything if that's what you're worried about."

"Wait—what? That's not—"

I kiss his cheek before he can finish. "See you around."

I get in Dad's car and start the engine, waiting a minute for the heat to kick on. As I drive off, I catch Briggs in the rearview mirror —frozen in the doorway, face scrunched in confusion, clearly not expecting me to shut him down.

Did I misread him? Was he hoping for more? Even if he were, nothing's changed. The timing is still wrong. Now, more than ever, we both need to stay focused.

It's early Sunday morning, and I don't pass a single car on the way to the Tide House in Founders Park.

I wonder where Lally spent the night. Did she go to River Birch, or is she with John Henry? Tears blur the road as I imagine what she must be going through. She has nothing left—not even a toothbrush.

When I arrive, Ben is standing on the Tide House dock, his gaze fixed on some distant point across the water.

I park and walk quietly out to join him, touching his jacket sleeve. "Hey. Are you okay? You're a million miles away."

He drops his head. "A million miles and twenty years. I was thinking about all the fun times we had here as kids. How hopeful we were about our future. Addie and I were so sure we'd grow old together." He shrugs. "No point reliving the past now."

I squeeze his arm. "I miss her too, Ben. Are you talking to anyone? A therapist?"

"Nah." He exhales slowly. "I'm doing something better. I'm making a change."

My brow furrows. "What kind of change?"

"I'm going to Florida. Hitting the road as soon as I leave here."

The shock sends a jolt through me, and I take a step back. "But Tidewell is your home."

He shakes his head. "Tidewell betrayed me, Lane. It stopped feeling like home a long time ago."

I nod. "I get that. How long will you be gone?"

A corner of his mouth lifts. "If I like it, maybe for good."

"What about your boat?"

"I found someone to rent it—to cover the dockage fee. At least until I decide if I'm staying in Florida." A flicker of excitement I haven't seen in a long time crosses his face. "I've been offered a job as a mate on a sport-fishing charter out of Bud and Mary's Marina in Islamorada."

"That's great, Ben. The change will do you good." I don't say how much I envy his clean escape.

His expression hardens. "I was on my boat the night Travis was killed. I saw you when you walked by on the dock."

"I saw you too—through the cabin window."

"I watched you leave the marina. You looked shaken, but not like someone who'd just murdered a man." He glances around before reaching into his coat and pulling out a manila envelope. "About five minutes later, Clay walked past. I waited a beat, then followed him out to Travis's boat."

My pulse spikes.

"I saw him drag Travis out of the salon onto the deck. I witnessed him hit Travis in the head with the butt of his pistol." Ben hands me the envelope. "I photographed everything. I texted the digital copies to your phone."

I undo the clasp and peer inside at the eight-by-ten photographs—five of them. Clear. Unmistakable. Damning.

"These are solid," I say quietly.

Ben's face reddens. "I'm sorry it took me so long to reach out. I didn't want to get involved. After everything I've been through, I was scared to step back into that mess. But I finally came to my senses. I can't let you go down for something you didn't do. I'll testify—if it comes to that."

I slide the photographs back into the envelope and hug it to my chest. "Is this why you're leaving town?"

He lifts a shoulder. "One reason. There are others."

I cup his cheek. "I wish you luck, my friend. If you ever need me, I'm here."

He pulls me into a hug. "Watch your back, Lane. The ground under your feet isn't solid anymore."

His words linger as I watch him drive away.

The evidence is solid. Irrefutable.

The question is: Who do I trust with it?

The short answer: nobody.

I weigh my few options as I drive back toward town, the envelope resting in my lap for safekeeping. I was hoping to avoid dragging Briggs into this. It'll be awkward after last night. But as the commonwealth's attorney, he's responsible for deciding what charges are filed and overseeing criminal prosecutions. He operates outside Boone's corrupt chain of command, and right now, he's the only one I can trust to do the right thing.

I swing by Briggs's house, but his Tahoe is gone. I continue on toward town. I'm headed to his office in the courthouse when I spot the Tahoe parked in front of the Captain's First Cup—an all-day breakfast diner.

I enter the diner and scan the sea of people. Briggs is seated at a table in the back, a stack of pancakes in front of him. Across from him, sipping a cup of coffee, is Alex.

Anger flashes through me, but I tamp it down just as quickly. I don't have time for Alex today. I steady myself, square my shoulders, and head their way. Whatever this is between them, I'm not turning around.

Briggs looks up, surprise flickering across his face.

"Lane," he says.

"Briggs." My gaze flicks to Alex before settling back on him. "Got a minute?"

He gestures toward Alex. "Can't it wait? We're in the middle of something."

I drag an empty chair from the next table and drop into it, setting the envelope between us. "You tell me. Do you think this can wait?"

He opens the envelope and slides out the stack of photographs. His blue eyes widen as he shuffles through them. "Is this what I think it is?"

"Yep." I lean back, arms crossed over my chest.

He flips through the photos once more, then returns them to the envelope, dropping it on the table. "Where'd you get these?"

I don't answer. Instead, I let my gaze drift to Alex.

She sets her coffee down slowly. "Excuse me. I need to use the restroom."

She's a journalist. She knows when to be discreet.

I wait until she's out of earshot. "Ben Holloway is the one who called me on your phone earlier. He lives on a boat at the marina, remember?"

"I remember," Briggs says curtly.

"He saw me come and go the night of Travis's murder. Right after I left, he spotted Clay heading out to Travis's boat. He followed him." I tap on the envelope. "He took these with his phone."

Briggs rakes his fingers through his hair, his pancakes forgotten. "This just got really ugly."

"No uglier than me getting suicided in Boone's jail," I say flatly.

He studies me, expression grim. "I can see the wheels spinning. What're you thinking?"

"We could reach out to Judge Carmichael over in Miller's Crossing again. But, like last time, Tate will make certain the case gets funneled right back to Tidewell."

Briggs nods. "And Clay walks on a second murder." He drums his fingers on the table. "I can have the state police make the arrest, but I still need a warrant."

I glance up as Alex exits the restroom and slides onto a stool at the bar. Mounted above her, a television plays footage from yesterday's press conference—my face framed by microphones, the chyron flashing across a national news network.

I sweep a hand toward the screen. "My sudden fame benefits

us. If we keep this fight local, the whole corrupt lot of them will hang themselves—on camera—right in front of the entire country."

Briggs watches the television for a long minute before turning back to me. "There's no way out for Clay this time. Should we go straight to Tate with the request for an arrest warrant?"

I shake my head. "We start with Boone. I want his head on the chopping block alongside Tate's." I stand abruptly.

"Where are you going?" Briggs pushes back from the table, pulling his wallet from his pocket.

I snatch up the envelope. "To see Boone."

He drops a wad of bills on the table. "Wait up, Lane. I'm coming with you."

I'm secretly pleased when he doesn't stop to speak with Alex on his way out.

Chapter Twenty-Eight

The desk officer at the sheriff's department informs us that Boone is at church.

"The early service at Tidewell Methodist. He goes every Sunday. Eight o'clock sharp," she says with a broad smile, as though proud of herself for knowing this information.

"He'll need all the prayers he can get when I'm done with him," I mutter as we turn away from her.

We're back in the Tahoe and rolling through quiet neighborhood streets. Most of the locals are tucked inside their homes—coffee brewing, blinds half drawn, nerves still raw from last night's fire.

Tidewell Methodist sits several blocks away on Maple Avenue, red brick and white columns, the kind of place that promises forgiveness without asking for too many details. Cars fill the lot, lined up neat and orderly.

Briggs slows as we pass. "What are we doing here? Waiting until he comes out?"

I spot Boone's cruiser angled near the front, gleaming like a badge of righteousness. "What choice do we have? If we leave and come back, we might miss him."

We park across the street and walk into the churchyard,

settling onto an iron bench to wait. From inside, hymn music rises, muffled but familiar. "Amazing Grace."

I huff a quiet breath. The irony is almost too on the nose.

"We should talk about last night while we're waiting," Briggs says.

"I can't even think about that now, Briggs." I put just enough edge on his name to make my meaning clear.

"Fine. Just so we're clear, it wasn't nothing to me."

I want to ask him where Alex fits in, but that would imply I care. And I totally care. But I don't dare let him know it.

I sit with that during the twenty-minute wait. I try not to think about last night—about being in his arms, about how right it felt. But the thoughts keep creeping in. We have chemistry. Electric. Edgy. Satisfying.

But passion rarely has staying power. At least not in my experience.

When the church doors finally open, Boone steps out into the sunlight, already slipping back into his public face—the genial sheriff, the man folks trust.

"There he is," I say, standing.

He spots us, and the color drains from his face.

Murmurs ripple through the crowd. I don't have to hear the words to know what they're saying. I'm no longer just a familiar face in Tidewell. I'm the detective who blew the lid off a reproductive trafficking ring.

And Boone knows it.

We wait for him to come to us. "You need to see me?" he asks, his gruff tone letting us know he's not happy about it.

"Yep. Is there somewhere we can talk?" My eyes travel to his wife, who's deep in conversation with the minister on the front steps. "If you want, we can follow you back to the station?"

Boone tracks my gaze. "She's got her own car. She can drive herself home." He shifts his weight. "But we'll talk here. I've got a tee time at eleven."

"Not anymore, you don't." I head toward the parking lot, sensing his stare burning into my back.

When we reach his cruiser, I pull the photographs from the envelope and hand them over.

His face tightens, his breathing shallow. "Who took these?"

I press my lips tight. "Can't say. He's willing to testify in court, but for now, I'm protecting his identity."

Boone fishes a pair of reading glasses from his blazer pocket and studies the photos. After a moment, he snorts. "They look photoshopped. Images of Clay could've been pulled straight from the internet."

I snatch the photographs back. "Don't even go there, Boone. You and I both know these are the real deal." I wave them at him. "Just like we both know Clay killed Addie."

Briggs checks his watch. "I can have the arrest warrant ready in an hour. I don't need your approval. But this thing is going to blow up the town. It'll play a lot better for your reelection campaign if you cooperate."

Boone grunts. "It's Sunday, Briggs. This can wait until tomorrow. Tate's out of town anyway."

"Liar." Briggs jerks his chin toward the street.

We all turn as Judge Tate crosses to his sedan, parked squarely in a No Parking—Loading Zone, as if the rules don't apply when you write them.

Boone turns back toward us. "I won't stand in your way. I'll let Tate know the request is coming and arrange for you to present it to him."

I tuck the packet of photographs under my arm. "You have until one o'clock, Boone. If Clay isn't in custody by then, I'm going to the press."

His face turns the angry red of a man used to being obeyed. "Are you threatening me?"

I step closer, lowering my voice. "In case you missed it, my face is all over the national news this morning. I'm the detective who took down Colt Craddock's human trafficking operation."

My eyes lock on his. "I'm not threatening you. I'm telling you how this is going to go. You tried to pin Travis Keene's murder on me without waiting for the autopsy results. You burned me—twice. There won't be a third time."

I hesitate, then add quietly, "And to think you were once my father's closest friend. Shame on you."

Boone lets out a slow breath through his nose. "You know . . . your daddy used to worry about you." His eyes turn cold. "Said you were gonna get yourself killed one day. Always sticking your nose where it didn't belong."

Something inside me goes still. "Careful, Boone. Sounds like *you're* threatening *me* now."

For a beat, Boone says nothing. The noise of churchgoers drifts around us—laughter, car doors, cheerful voices making brunch plans.

Finally, he looks away. "You'll have your warrant by one."

I shake my head. "No, Boone. Clay needs to be in custody by one. Make a note of it, in case you forget."

Boone's jaw tightens. He mutters something I can't make out, climbs into his cruiser, and pulls away, gravel spitting beneath his tires.

"You were reckless before, Lane. But that?" Briggs shakes his head. "That was a death wish."

"Don't worry about it, Briggs. I can take care of myself." I turn away, then remember we rode together. "Can you take me back to my car?"

His expression softens. "Of course. Aren't you going to help me draft the warrant request?"

"I can't. I have other commitments. My friend . . . my *girlfriend*, is waiting for me."

I climb into the Tahoe, setting the manila envelope on his console. "You'll need these. Guard them with your life."

He eyes the envelope as he starts the engine. "I'll make copies and put the originals in my office safe." He pulls out of the parking lot onto the road. "What you said to Boone back there about him burning you twice. Once was Keene's murder. What was the other time?"

I stare out the window, my breath fogging up the glass. "Something that happened a very long time ago." I keep my eyes on the window. "He knows."

Briggs waits for me to say more. When I remain silent, he doesn't press.

"What happens if Clay isn't locked up by one?" he asks.

"Just what I said. I'll call a press conference."

He glances over at me. "Do you even know how to call a press conference?"

"No, Briggs. I don't. You can ask Alex to handle it. She loves the limelight."

"I'll let you be the one to ask her," he says, wheeling into the parking space next to my Bronco.

I open the door to get out. "By the way, I don't have my phone with me." I pull out my burner phone and shoot him a text. "You can reach me at this number."

"Be careful, Lane," he calls after me.

"I always am." I slam the door.

Why am I so mad at him? Or am I just mad at myself—for being vulnerable, for liking him too much. Vulnerability has never been a luxury I can afford.

Unlocking Dad's car, I slide behind the wheel, start the engine, and send Caroline an email, letting her know I'm on my way.

She's waiting at the door with her bags packed when I arrive forty-five minutes later.

"Take me there, Lane." She grabs my hands and squeezes. "Please. I can't stand this waiting. I need to find my embabies."

The firm set of her jaw and the intensity in her green eyes tell me she won't let this go.

I sigh. "Have you tried calling the fertility clinic in Richmond?"

"Yes!" Her voice wavers. "But no one answered. They're not open on the weekends."

After all she's been through, I can't possibly deny her this. I glance at the clock on the mantle. It's ten thirty. If we hurry, we can stop by The Overlook on the way back to Tidewell.

"Okay. I'll take you. But we don't have much time. Some stuff is happening today. I'll tell you about it on the way. Let me shower and pack my things. I'll be down in a minute."

She follows me to the stairs. "Are you hungry? I can make you an omelet."

"Starving," I call down to her. "But let's just grab something on the road."

Despite the rush, I take extra time to dry my hair and put on some makeup. I don't hold out much hope that Tate will come through with the arrest warrant, and I want to look my best for my encore appearance on the national news.

Caroline orders takeout from the CarWash Café in Kilmarnock —a buttery croissant stuffed with scrambled eggs, cheese, and sausage. Delicious. And nearly impossible to eat while driving.

"Tell me what stuff is happening today," she says, gathering our trash.

"I can't say much. It's an ongoing investigation. But evidence that clears me of Travis Keene's murder charges has surfaced. My friend, Lawson Briggs—the commonwealth's attorney—is drafting the arrest warrant now. Sheriff Boone has until one o'clock to take the suspect into custody."

"Is Lawson more than a friend?"

My head jerks toward her. She's wearing a mischievous grin that makes her eyes twinkle. "Why do you ask that?"

"Your face went all soft when you mentioned him." She runs a finger along my cheek. "That glow is a dead giveaway."

I return my attention to the road. I'm not used to talking about feelings like this. "It's complicated."

"Then uncomplicate it. You deserve happiness, Lane—after all you do for everyone else."

"Let's just focus on getting your embabies back." I turn up the volume on the police scanner. "Sorry about the static, but I'm waiting to hear if they send a unit to arrest the suspect."

She waves me off. "No worries at all. I'm not very good company right now anyway."

We ride for a while in silence, each of us lost in our own thoughts. I imagine what Caroline's life will look like if she never recovers her embryos—how hard it will be to move forward without the husband and children she once believed were her future. She's a lovely young woman with much to offer. She'll find happiness again.

Or maybe she won't. I certainly haven't. Then again, my situation is different. My husband betrayed me. It's hard to trust anyone again after your spouse—the person you vowed to spend the rest of your life with—tosses you aside without looking back.

That's the truth I don't say out loud. And the reason I keep pushing Briggs away.

I cast frequent glances at the dashboard clock, watching the minutes tick toward the appointed hour. A sick feeling settles in my gut. Tate will deny the arrest warrant, and I'll have no choice but to act on my threat. The national networks will jump at the chance to follow up on today's top story. I'd rather not involve Alex, but how else would I even reach them?

My problem solves itself when I see the press already gathered outside the auxiliary building at The Overlook.

It's twelve fifteen.

Forty-five minutes until the fireworks.

Chapter Twenty-Nine

Reporters call out as we make our way from the car to the barn.

"Ignore them," I tell Caroline. "Keep your head down."

The kidnapped women have already been removed from the facility. The place is still crawling with state police, but there are new faces now as well—federal agents, calm and methodical, already treating the place like a long-term crime scene.

I don't need my credentials for identification. A murmur follows us as we enter—my name, whispered, recognized from the news. A trooper at the door glances at Caroline, then back at me, and steps aside without a word.

We head straight for the cryogenic lab, where a team of technicians in white coats is busy at work. Moving among them, clipboard in hand, is the same crime-scene tech from yesterday.

When she spots me, she waves us over. I introduce her to Caroline. "This is the woman I mentioned yesterday. I'm sorry, I didn't catch your name."

"Lila Burnett." She smiles softly at Caroline. "Nice to meet you. The team from Commonwealth Reproductive Institute in Richmond has taken over, and they are making progress in cracking the code." She gestures across the lab. "Rebecca Kingsley —the one with dark hair—is leading the team."

Rebecca stands a few feet away, her eyes glued to a laptop as data scrolls across the screen.

"She knows about you," Lila adds. "She can give you the latest updates."

Caroline smiles softly. "Thank you so much."

"Of course. I wish you luck in finding your embryos." She spreads her arms wide. "This has all been . . . very humbling, to say the least."

Caroline and I weave our way through the controlled chaos toward Rebecca.

I cough to clear my throat. "Excuse me. If I could interrupt for a minute."

Rebecca looks up, and her brown eyes widen. "You're Lane Sutherlin—from the news."

I nod. "And this is Caroline Edwards."

Her expression softens as she turns toward Caroline. "I'm so sorry for everything you've been through."

Caroline clasps her hands together. "Thank you. Do you have an update regarding my embryos?"

Rebecca nods. "Actually, yes. We're pretty sure we've identi-fied yours. Each egg and embryo was logged with a donor code— scrubbed of names but not of origin data. We matched the code to the hormone profile and retrieval date from your clinic records. Then we confirmed it with the storage medium they were preserved in. It's a long shot most of the time." Her lips part in a small smile. "But in your case, the data lined up."

Caroline's breath catches. "You said you're pretty sure? How can we be positive?"

"We'll confirm it with DNA. We should have the results in a few days." She pauses, as though choosing her words carefully. "Tomorrow morning, we'll transfer all the eggs and embryos to our lab in Richmond. If everything goes smoothly, we can move quickly toward implantation. It's possible you could be pregnant by Christmas."

Caroline sways slightly as the last of her strength drains from her. She leans into me, and I place a steadying hand on her back.

"Thank you," she whispers. "I didn't think this would ever happen."

Rebecca squeezes her shoulder. "I'm glad it worked out." She presses a business card into her hand. "Call the clinic first thing in the morning. I'll alert the front desk. We'll take good care of you."

My burner phone vibrates. One o'clock sharp. My stomach knots as I step away to take the call.

"Boone hasn't moved," Briggs says when I answer. "Tate's still sitting on the arrest warrant. They're testing you, Lane."

"Then it's time to raise the stakes."

"Judge Carmichael in Miller's Crossing is on standby. He went ballistic when I told him about the photos. He's more than happy to issue the arrest warrant."

Relief flickers through me but only briefly. "Good. I'm at The Overlook. The press is already here, and they're hungry. They will eat this up."

"What are you thinking, Lane?" he asks, skepticism threading his voice.

"Get the warrant from Carmichael. But hold the state police for thirty minutes. I want this to unfold where everyone can see it."

He exhales. "You're turning this into a pressure cooker."

"Not me. They did that. I'm just taking the lid off," I say, ending the call.

I glance at Caroline—still clutching Rebecca's card like it might disappear if she lets go. Her face is alight with relief, joy breaking through layers of grief and fear. She deserves this moment after everything those men put her through.

More than that—she deserves to be heard.

I return to them, my fingers grazing Caroline's arm. "The reporters are outside. I'm sure they would love to hear from you.

What this did to you, what was taken, and what it means to get it back. Reproductive trafficking is on the rise, Caroline. Your story might help other women avoid the same heartache."

Caroline doesn't hesitate. "You're right. They need to know."

"Do you want a minute first?"

She draws a shaky breath, pulling herself to her full height. "No. Let's go now, before I lose my nerve."

Five minutes later, we're standing at the podium together. I nudge her forward, and she taps the mic. She's a concert pianist—comfortable in front of a live audience.

"I'm Caroline Edwards, and I'd like to share my story. After years of trying, my husband and I were finally going to have our baby . . . *babies*—a boy and a girl. The doctor was preparing to implant our fertilized embryos when I got word my husband had been killed in a car accident."

She pauses, steadying herself.

"A couple of months later, the grief eased enough for me to realize I could still have a version of the future we'd dreamed of. That he could live on through his children. The night before my scheduled procedure, the Willow Creek Clinic caught fire."

A hand shoots up in the crowd. "Are you Caroline Edwards, the concert pianist?"

A ripple moves through the reporters. Cameras shift. Lenses tighten.

"Yes. And my husband was Dr. Julian Edwards—a neurologist. He was well known in his field." She steadies herself. "But at the end of the day, we were just another couple who couldn't conceive a child."

She looks directly into the cameras. "What happened to me can happen to anyone. If you're a woman who has frozen eggs or fertilized embryos—ask questions. Demand records. Don't assume the system is protecting you."

Her voice trembles, but she doesn't stop.

"I trusted a clinic with the most precious thing I had left of my husband. And someone decided they had a right to take it." Caroline's gaze hardens with resolve. "I'm telling my story so other women don't have to go through what I've been through. So other women don't miss out on their last chance to give birth to their biological children."

She glances over at me. "I was fortunate. A nurse at the Willow Creek Clinic introduced me to Detective Lane Sutherlin." Her voice breaks. "Lane risked her life to find my embryos." Tears stream down Caroline's face. "I don't know how I can ever repay you."

The reporters pivot as one, lenses swinging in my direction. Caroline steps aside, and I take the podium.

"What's next for you, Detective?" a reporter calls out.

I grip the sides of the podium. "Clearing my name."

A murmur ripples through the crowd.

"Evidence was delivered to me this morning that directly implicates another suspect in the murder of Travis Keene," I continue. "That evidence has been reviewed by Tidewell's commonwealth's attorney."

"Who's the suspect?" someone shouts.

"I'm not prepared to divulge that information yet," I say evenly. "But I can tell you this—he's a member of Tidewell's elite society. The Old Guard."

The murmurs swell—louder now. Edgier.

"The commonwealth's attorney presented the arrest request to Judge Vernon Tate earlier this morning." I pause for effect. "And he has chosen not to act."

Reporters talk over one another. Cameras zoom in. Red lights blink.

"Let me be very clear," I continue, my voice steady as I lock onto the nearest camera. "If this suspect is not taken into custody today, it will not be because of a lack of evidence. It will be because the system failed—again."

I lean into the podium. "I did not kill Travis Keene. I was framed because I got too close to the truth. And the same people who tried to silence me are counting on the public to look away." I scan the crowd. "I'm not looking away. And neither should you."

I turn away from the podium, whispering to Caroline, "Come on. Let's go."

We weave past the cameras and shouting reporters, moving fast now, until we're back in the car and pulling away from The Overlook. The noise fades in the rearview mirror, replaced by the steady hum of the road.

Caroline exhales a long, shaky breath. "You were incredible up there, Lane. But I'm terrified for you. Your life is in danger."

"I'm more worried about you," I say, eyes fixed on the road. "Once this arrest goes down, things could get unpredictable. But you'll be safe at River Birch."

She tugs her coat tighter around her. "I appreciate that. But I need to get out of your hair. I'm going to head back to Richmond this afternoon. I want to be there in the morning. I'm hoping to get in to see a doctor at the new fertility clinic first thing."

"I don't blame you." I signal toward the turnoff. "And truthfully, you'll be safer in Richmond. Although maybe you should stay with your dad for a couple of days."

She nods. "He's staying with me, actually. We've already made a plan."

We don't speak after that. The silence isn't awkward—just heavy with everything we don't say.

When I pull up in front of River Birch, Caroline turns to me, her green eyes shining. "I don't know how I'll ever thank you. You gave me back my future. You gave me a reason to live."

I shake my head. "You did that yourself. I just helped you find it."

We get out of the car and transfer her luggage to her Range Rover.

I gesture at my brother's pickup. "Judd's here. He'll help you with the rest of your luggage. I hate to cut out on you, but I really need to get to town."

"I understand." She wraps her arms around me, holding on tight. For a moment, neither of us moves.

I push away, holding her at arm's length. "When this is over—when it's safe—I hope you'll come back for a visit."

She smiles softly. "I'd love that. Or you can come visit me at our place next summer." She cups my cheek. "Be careful, Lane."

"I will. Text me when you get home," I say, swallowing past the lump in my throat.

Instead of returning to Dad's Volvo, I climb into my Bronco. I no longer care who follows me. I've got the press on my side now.

I grab my phone from the cup holder and scroll through two days of missed calls and unanswered texts, relieved to find Ben's message with the images attached. I save them to my phone, then forward everything to my Gmail account. Insurance.

Saying goodbye to Caroline leaves a hollow ache in my chest as I pull away from River Birch. Hope looks good on her. I wish it were that simple for me.

I merge onto the road toward Tidewell, the sky darkening ahead, the town waiting like it always does—tight-lipped and dangerous. I savor this moment of borrowed calm.

Borrowed things never last.

Chapter Thirty

I arrive at Clay Dalton's house to find state and local law enforcement locked in a standoff that has nothing to do with Clay and everything to do with ego.

Boone is planted near the front steps, hands on hips, jaw working like he's chewing glass. Across from him stands an uptight-looking man in a starched uniform, shoes polished to a mirror shine. His name tag reads Jameson, and he carries himself like he hasn't lost an argument in years—a Virginia State Police Special Agent sent to make sure this arrest happens by the book.

Briggs leans against a porch railing, arms crossed, lips curved in something dangerously close to smug. His head jerks back and forth as if he's watching a ping-pong match—Boone, Jameson, Boone again.

"Judge Carmichael issued the warrant first," Jameson says, his tone crisp and final. He holds up the paperwork like a badge of honor. "That gives the Virginia State Police primary jurisdiction."

Boone bristles. "I don't care who issued the blasted warrant first. This is my town, and I'm taking him in."

Jameson doesn't blink. "Your town doesn't outrank a lawful warrant."

I slide in beside Brody Talcott. "What's going on?"

Brody glances over at me. "There's a dispute over who gets the arrest."

Briggs examines his fingernails. "See that, Sheriff? Looks like the rules matter after all."

Boone's glare could strip paint. "You went behind my back."

Briggs drops his hand and pushes himself off the railing. "Correction. I went around corruption."

Silence settles over the crowd.

My gaze sweeps the property. Clay's truck sits in the driveway. Shades drawn. Front door closed. "Where's Clay?"

Brody lowers his voice. "He locked himself inside. He's refusing to come out. Says we'll have to break down the door."

My pulse kicks. "Then why are we standing here arguing?"

I push my way to the front of the crowd, flashing my badge at Jameson. "Detective Lane Sutherlin. I've been consulting on this investigation." It's a stretch but not an outright lie. I keep talking before anyone can stop me. "I was close to Clay's wife. I know firsthand that he's a gun collector—he's got a full-blown arsenal in there. He's also paranoid, and with his house surrounded, he's likely to go off like a lit cannon."

Boone looks down his nose at me. "Get lost, Sutherlin. You have no jurisdiction here."

I ignore him, my attention on the special agent. "Clay is also a flight risk. When we arrested him for his wife's murder, he didn't go quietly." I gesture toward the house. "While we're standing here arguing, he could already be making a break out the back."

Jameson's jaw tightens. He lifts his shoulder mic. "Stand by for tactical. We're not waiting this out."

Boone opens his mouth. "But—"

Jameson cuts him off without looking. "This is no longer a jurisdictional issue. It's an officer-safety issue. Clear the area. We're going in."

A wave of state police swarm the house at once. The front door explodes inward with a concussive crack, wood splintering as the tactical team pours into the house in a controlled rush—weapons trained, voices sharp and overlapping.

"State police! Show me your hands!"

I hide with Brody behind a patrol car as the noise swallows the house—boots pounding, orders barked, a crash from overturned furniture.

Then someone shouts. "He's on the move!"

Seconds stretch. My pulse hammers.

Then—"Suspect down!"

Moments later, they drag Clay out of the house, wrists zip-tied behind his back, face flushed with rage and disbelief. One sleeve of his flannel shirt is ripped, a thin line of blood running from his temple.

Jameson steps forward. "Clay Dalton, you're under arrest for the murder of Travis Keene."

Clay bucks against the officers as they march him toward the waiting cruiser. His wild eyes rake the crowd before locking on me. "You bitch," he snarls. "You'll pay for this. Your lame evidence will be thrown out on a technicality."

I don't raise my voice. I don't need to. "We'll see about that, Clay. Jury tampering is off the table for this murder trial."

He throws his head back and laughs—a sharp, unhinged sound. "Don't count on it."

"I'd advise you to keep your mouth shut, Dalton," the arresting officer says, shoving him into the back seat and slamming the door.

"Where are you taking him?" I call out.

Before Jameson can answer, Boone steps in. "Get lost, Sutherlin."

He turns to Jameson, his voice ironclad, "He stays in Tidewell. Take him to the sheriff's department."

Jameson hesitates a beat before giving a reluctant nod.

My stomach drops.

I grab Boone's arm, spinning him toward me. "Seriously, Boone. You and I both know that's a mistake."

His eyes harden. "The crime happened here. The trial will happen here too. Briggs had no business getting Judge Carmichael involved."

"We warned you we wouldn't wait." I step closer, lowering my voice so only he can hear. "When you lie down with dogs, you get up with fleas."

Something flickers across his face—irritation, maybe guilt—but it's gone just as fast.

"What happened to you, Boone?" I ask softly. "Where's the man I used to love? My father's best friend. My Uncle Franklin. The man who came over every Saturday night for cookouts. Who carried me around on his shoulders like I was the daughter he never had."

His facial muscles tighten, a vein at his temple pulsing. "Law enforcement is nasty business, Sutherlin," he says flatly.

"Only if you let the bad guys take control," I fire back. "If you're weak. If you're greedy. If you care more about power than justice."

For a long moment, we stare at each other—history, choices, consequences hanging thick between us.

"When did it happen, Uncle Frank? What made you change?"

Agony contorts his face. His chin hits his chest. "It started with Tommy's accident. There's so much you don't know, Lane." He looks up at me, his blue eyes glassy. "And the deeper you dig, the closer to danger you become." He steps closer, lowering his voice. "A word of warning—from someone who once loved you. Get out while you can."

I shake my head. "I'm not a quitter. I walked away once, and it nearly destroyed me." I glance at his badge. "I'm not walking away again."

I turn away from him and go in search of Brody, pulling him aside. "Clay's not safe in your jail. But you already know that. Put him on suicide watch."

He lets out a breath. "I don't have that authority, Lane. I'm already on the outside looking in."

"Do what you can." I slap his back. "Hang on a little longer, buddy. Things are about to change."

He gives me a look. "And who's going to change them? You?"

The answer lands in my chest before finding my lips. "Someone has to."

As I walk away, the truth settles over me—quiet, steady, undeniable.

This is what I've been fighting for. It's about more than finding justice for Addie's murder, or busting up a human trafficking operation, or clearing my name. It's about more than exposing corruption and giving the town back to its citizens.

I was never cut out to sit behind a bench and pass judgment.

But standing in the trenches—holding the line—is in my blood.

I've been circling this truth since I came back to town.

I don't just want justice—I want the job.

I'm following in my father's footsteps.

Lane Sutherlin style.

Chapter Thirty-One

I return to my Bronco to find Wylie Craddock leaning against the front fender, smoking a cigarette, perfectly at ease where he has no business being.

"Put that nasty thing out," I say, waving a hand in front of my nose.

"Wanna make me?" He pushes off the Bronco, unfolding to his full height. He's taller than six feet—closer to six and a half—and he looms over me, clearly expecting me to cower.

I don't. I square my shoulders and hold my chin high. "You mean like yesterday?" I sweep an arm toward the uniforms milling around the street. "You want me to embarrass you again in front of all these people?"

His mouth twitches. Not a smile. A calculation.

He takes one last drag and grinds the cigarette into the pavement with his boot. "You caught me off guard yesterday." He drags his menacing eyes over me, slow and deliberate. "I didn't know you had such impressive skills."

I shift my weight, ready. "What do you want, Craddock?"

He steps closer. Too close. I can smell cigarette smoke and something sharper—anger, maybe. Or fear dressed up as arrogance.

"To pass along a message." He leans in. "Watch your back, Sutherlin. You're a dead woman."

I roll my eyes. "More empty threats. Can't you come up with something more original?"

"Empty is an illusion. A tactical maneuver. We're going for the slow-burn approach. We'll make you so paranoid in your own skin that, by the time we make good on those threats, you'll be begging us to kill you."

My stomach churns, but I keep my face neutral. "You think my karate skills were impressive. Wait until you see how precise I am with a gun."

His eyes darken with pure hate. "Bring it on, Sutherlin. I'm not worried."

I should walk away. But I need to keep him talking to find out how much he's willing to give away.

I fold my arms over my chest, tapping the toe of my boot on the pavement. "What's this really about, Craddock? You boys have had so many setbacks recently, it's hard to know. Is it retaliation for taking down Colt's operation? Or is it Clay's arrest? You thought you'd get away with another murder."

He steps closer. "Leave Colt out of this. He was never one of us. We had nothing to do with his trafficking operation. Truthfully, I find the whole thing distasteful."

I don't ask who *us* is. I already know. "What about his son, Colter? He's one of you—king of the Night Ryders."

"Colter is a good boy, loyal to his father like any honorable son should be," Wylie says smoothly. "But he wasn't involved in that operation either."

The state cruiser crawls past, Clay slumped in the back seat, head bowed as he stares at his lap.

Wylie watches them go. "As for Clay? He's an idiot. He gets what he deserves."

"What's he gonna get, Wylie? You taking him out in jail?"

He shrugs, casual as a man discussing the weather. "Not my

call." He pauses, stroking his scruff. "Not a bad idea, though. We could use a fall guy right about now."

My pulse kicks. "Why are you telling me this?"

He reaches up, fingers brushing my cheek.

I slap his hand away, hard.

"Why do you think? Because we have no intention of letting you live." He opens my car door with mock courtesy. "I believe you were leaving. Wouldn't want to hold you up." He tilts his head, smiling. "I didn't tamper with your car. Or did I?"

He makes a low boom sound under his breath. Childish. Cruel.

My heart hammers, but I don't let it show. I slide behind the wheel. "You wouldn't dare. Not with this many law enforcement officers on the scene."

I make a show of pushing the start button, but my heart is pounding, and I'm relieved when the engine turns over with no explosion.

"You're right. We wouldn't want an audience." He leans closer. "Maybe it's a time device—set to go off in five minutes. Maybe ten. Maybe twenty—right about the time you pull into River Birch."

He straightens and taps the roof once. "Have a lovely day, sweetheart."

I pull out without looking back.

I weave my way through town—blowing through yellow lights, rolling stop signs, passing the boardwalk, the marina, the resort, and Captain's Row without slowing. I don't stop until I'm in the country, where the road narrows and trees close in. Far from civilization. If the Bronco explodes, only I will die.

I jump out and drop to the ground, crawling beneath the vehicle. Using the flashlight on my phone, I scan the undercarriage inch by inch, my pulse roaring in my ears.

When I'm convinced there's nothing there, I pop the hood and check the engine. Then the interior—under the seats, behind the panels, every place someone could hide something small and deadly. Nothing.

I slump back against the Bronco, the metal still warm beneath my palms, and force myself to breathe. This just got real. And dangerous. And I'm no longer the only one paying the price.

On my way back to town, I detour through the Captain's Row neighborhood. Guilt grips my chest when I spot Lally moving slowly through the charred remains of what was once her home. The air still smells faintly of smoke and wet ash. Blackened studs jut toward the sky like broken ribs.

I recognize the bucket she's carrying—ours, from the laundry room—and the boots on her feet, scuffed and familiar, are Dad's. She must've found them in the mudroom.

The loss hits me all at once. Every single thing she owned gone —her rain boots, her photo albums of her children through the ages, a lifetime reduced to debris.

I approach quietly, not wanting to startle her. She's a million miles away, kneeling in the rubble, fishing a lightbulb from the ashes. She turns it over in her hand like it might still matter, then drops it into the bucket with a dull clink.

Her hand flies to her chest when she finally notices me. "Lord, child," she says breathless. "You scared me to death. I was so lost in thought I didn't hear you."

I promised myself I'd keep it together. I don't.

The tears come fast and hard as I cross the distance between us and fling my arms around her. "Lally," I choke out. "I'm so, so sorry. This is all my fault. You lost your house—everything you own—because of me."

She drops the bucket and wraps her arms around me, holding me tight. "Hush now, sweet girl," she says softly. "You're talking nonsense. You were doing your job—trying to save our town. Sacrifices will have to be made. I'm just grateful no one was hurt."

I wipe my face on her dress before lifting my head. "You're too good to me."

She cups my cheek. "You're my family, Lane Sutherlin. You,

your daddy, Judd, Brandy." She pats her chest. "I love you in my heart just the same as I love my own children."

"But your house—"

"I have insurance. I'll rebuild in time," she says calmly. "A smaller house. One more suited to my stage of life. For now, I'm needed at River Birch to help care for your daddy. Some things in this life happen for a reason."

Wylie's threat echoes in my mind. Everyone close to me is in danger.

"Given the circumstances, you might be safer staying with John Henry."

"John Henry doesn't need me," she says without hesitation. "Your daddy does. I've made up my mind. I'm staying at River Birch."

"If you insist." I spread my arms wide at the wreckage. "At least let me help you here. What're you looking for?"

She gives her head a bewildered shake. "Nothing in particular. Anything worth salvaging."

We move slowly, carefully, as if the ruins might still be hot enough to burn us. The house is reduced to blackened beams and warped metal, the smell of smoke baked into everything. I nudge aside a collapsed cabinet with my boot.

"There," Lally says, pointing. Half buried in ash is a ceramic mixing bowl, its rim chipped but intact. The blue cornflower pattern is barely visible beneath the soot. She gently lifts it from the rubble. "It was my mama's. I used it every Sunday when making biscuits."

I swallow past the lump in my throat. "It's pretty."

Lally nods. "It is." She runs her finger along the chipped rim. "At least it was."

We find cutlery and pewter cups and a warped picture frame, the glass gone but the backing intact. A cast-iron skillet, blackened but whole. A watch with a cracked face, stopped at eight thirty— around the time of the fire. A shoe buckle, Lally's good Sunday brooch, and her silver locket—now tarnished, but the photos of her two oldest grandchildren are still intact.

I'm sifting through a pile of burned clothes when my pocket vibrates. I tug out my phone. A text from an unknown number.

The world tilts beneath me when I see the attached photo.

I pocket my phone.

"I'm sorry, Lally. I need to get home." I pull her into a quick hug.

She frowns. "Is everything okay?"

My gut tightens. "I'm not sure, honestly. Things are heating up with this case. I really wish you'd reconsider and stay at John Henry's."

Lally gives her head an adamant shake. "No, Lane. My decision is final." She drops the bucket and wipes her sooty hands on her dress. "I'm done here for today anyway. I'll stop at the grocery store and pick up something for dinner. I'll be home in a bit."

I lift the bucket and take hold of her arm. "Don't worry about groceries," I say, steering her toward her car. "We'll figure dinner out later. There's plenty to eat in the freezer. For now, I want you close to me."

She stops short and wrenches her arm free. "What is it, Lane? You're scaring me."

"Because *I'm* scared, Lally. That's why I want you at John Henry's. These are dangerous men we're up against."

She keeps walking to her car, retrieves her purse from the passenger seat, and turns back to me. "I can take care of myself." She opens the purse just enough for me to see the small pistol nestled inside.

"John Henry taught me how to use it," she says proudly. "I'm a pretty good shot, if I say so myself."

My eyes widen. "How long have you had that?"

She closes the purse and tucks it under her arm. "I'm not exactly sure. A long time. A couple of decades at least. Your daddy gave me the money and told me exactly what to buy. With him being a judge, he felt everyone around him needed to know how to protect themselves."

I smile. "That sounds like him."

Dusk settles over the fields as I pull back onto the road. Everyone I love is arming themselves. Everyone is bracing. I tighten my grip on the wheel and head for home.

Their message is clear.

One thing is certain.

They're done warning me.

Chapter Thirty-Two

I speed home with one eye on Lally's van in the rearview mirror. Coming up from behind—a black dot on the horizon—is Shadow Man.

Ugh. I palm the steering wheel. I'm so sick of these guys.

At home, I hurry Lally inside and race through the house, checking every window and door, making sure they're locked. Judd finds me minutes later in Dad's study, rummaging through the gun safe.

"What's going on, Lane?" Concern roughens his voice, like he already knows something bad has happened, but he's afraid to hear it out loud.

I pull out Dad's semi-automatic rifle and close the safe. I've been debating whether to tell him the truth, but he needs to know. To protect himself. His wife. Their unborn child.

I shut the study door and gesture to the loveseat. "Sit down."

He lowers himself to the edge of the cushion. I take Dad's recliner and tell him everything—my confrontation with Wylie, the threat, the warning.

"And then they sent me this."

I hold out my phone.

Judd's breath catches as he stares at the image—a photograph of Dad, Judd, and Brandy on the back patio. The photo has been doctored. A bullet is superimposed beside Dad's head. A noose hangs around Judd's neck. A red circle is drawn around Brandy's belly. No message. None is needed.

The color drains from my brother's face, and I hang my head. "I'm *so* sorry I brought this on our family," I say quietly. "It's a long shot, but I might be able to get you, Brandy, and Dad into WITSEC temporarily."

I'd have to beg Morales, and I'm not even sure he has that kind of pull. Why would the government be willing to spend hundreds of thousands of dollars to protect Judd and Brandy when they have nothing to offer in return?

"Where does it end, Lane?" he asks, his voice unsteady, eyes still locked on the photo.

"Where I believe it began." I swallow hard. "With Tommy's accident. Wylie had something to do with his death, and Boone covered it up." I meet his gaze. "I'm going after them, Judd. It won't be pretty. But if it's the last thing I do, I will make them pay."

"Do you have a plan?" His expression is intent. He's not mocking me.

"Not yet. But I have leads." I take a breath. "I'll start with Boone. All roads lead back to him. As long as he's in control, none of us are safe."

"And the militia—the Night Ryders?"

"I'll take them out one at a time if necessary." I get to my feet and start pacing. "Tate's a problem, too, but Judge Carmichael in Miller's Crossing is on our side."

I stop pacing, the truth settling into my chest. "I don't have it all figured out yet. I need time."

Judd jabs his finger at the phone screen. "This pic could be just another fake—Wylie making good on his threat to mess with your head."

I shrug. "Could be. Probably is. But are you willing to take that chance?"

I lift my right arm, the rifle angled toward the ceiling. "Five people live here now. One has dementia. One is pregnant. And one just lost her home because of them."

Judd exhales slowly. "We're not the only ones suffering in Tidewell, Lane. People are scared." He looks at me differently now—steady, resolved. "Friends of mine have come to me. Good men. They want to get involved, to take action. I've put them off until now because the timing wasn't right." He hands me back my phone. "This changes things."

I shake my head. "Careful, Judd. We can't have a bunch of vigilantes running around town like loose cannons."

"They're not amateurs. Most of them grew up together. Eagle Scouts. Lifelong hunters. Veterans." His jaw tightens. "They're ordinary people who wanted quiet lives. Boone and the Old Guard took that away from them." He doesn't raise his voice. He doesn't need to. "And when men like that decide they've had enough—it's not chaos. It's war."

His words chill me, and I stumble back to Dad's chair. "I don't know, Judd. What you're suggesting is too risky. I'm a law enforcement officer. I'm sworn to uphold the law."

He cocks an eyebrow. "Really? Last time I checked, you weren't employed by any agency with jurisdiction in Tidewell."

I start to argue, but he kneels beside the chair before I can, bringing his voice down, making me listen. "I've held these guys off as long as I can. They're going after the Old Guard, Lane, with or without us. What they need is someone smart steering the ship."

My pulse hammers. "You mean me."

"I mean you," he says evenly. "You can organize us. Direct us. Plug us in where we're needed—and pull us back when we're not."

I blink hard. "*We? Us?*" The words taste dangerous.

His mouth quirks, but there's no humor in it. "I'm all in. A hundred percent. I'm going to raise my child in Tidewell, come hell or high water. Which means someone's gotta go. And it won't be me. But we can't do this alone. Not without you."

I rest my head against the back of the chair. "This is a huge decision. I need to sleep on it." I pause, then add, "But my mind is already turning over ways they could be useful."

Judd straightens. "I'll need your answer in the morning." He meets my gaze, steady and resolved. "They're ready, Lane. And whether or not you step in, this is moving forward. I'd rather have you leading it."

———

When the others retire for the night, I settle into the chair beside the French doors with the semi-automatic rifle across my lap. Shawna's chair. We'll have to let her go—temporarily. I refuse to put another innocent person in harm's way.

Sleep doesn't come. I knew it wouldn't. But I'll manage. I'm conditioned by overnight stakeouts, by waiting in the dark with nothing but instinct and adrenaline to keep me alert.

My thoughts drift to Judd's army—how I would lead them, how to keep them alive while accomplishing what needs to be done. I could teach them tactical movement, assess their marksmanship, push their physical limits. No one goes front line without earning it. The rest would be assigned where they can do the least harm—and the most good.

It's risky. But it's doable. And it might be the only way to protect my family.

At some point during the night, exhaustion wins.

The doorbell jolts me awake early Monday morning. Before I can rise from my chair, I hear the alarm being disarmed and low voices in the front hall. Lally's. And . . . is that Briggs?

I move to the edge of the chair, leaning closer to listen. They're talking about long-ago times—when Tommy was alive and Briggs practically lived at River Birch.

When their footsteps grow louder, I scramble up and slide the gun beneath the sofa.

"Look what the cat dragged in," Lally says, beaming.

I give him a curt nod. "Morning. I wasn't expecting you."

"I have news about the case." Briggs eyes the patio doors. "Is there somewhere we can talk?"

I follow his gaze, mentally cataloging sight lines and exits. We'll be safer away from the house. "We can walk down to the water."

"Let me fix you some coffee to take with you," Lally says, already bustling toward the kitchen.

When Briggs follows her, I retrieve the rifle from beneath the sofa and hurry down the hall to the gun safe in Dad's study. I swap it for two pistols and a buck knife—one gun riding my hip, the other secured in a shoulder holster, the blade tucked beneath my pant leg.

I bolt upstairs to brush my teeth, and when I return, Briggs is waiting with two coffees in hand.

As we stroll down the driveway, Briggs marvels at the row of river birch trees. "I haven't been out here since your father planted these trees, the summer after Tommy died. Hard to believe they've grown so tall. Then again, it's been nineteen years."

"Nineteen years of secrets and unanswered questions," I mutter.

He tilts his head, leaning closer. "Say again. I didn't hear you."

"Never mind," I say, eyes on the gravel road ahead. "So you have news about the case?"

He stops walking. "They found Clay dead in his cell this morning. Looks like an overdose."

My stomach lurches. For a second, I think I might be sick. Not because Clay is dead—he had it coming—but because it was so damn predictable. And no one listened when I tried to stop it. "Just like they did to Ben. This time they succeeded."

"Boone says there's no evidence of foul play."

I look at him like he's lost his mind. "Seriously, Briggs? Are you surprised?"

Briggs kicks at a rock. "No. You called it. I just didn't think they'd be that bold."

I shake my head in disgust. "Clay was their fall guy, just like Wylie said."

Lines appear on Brigg's forehead. "Wait. When did Wylie call Clay a fall guy? Were those his exact words?"

I scan the perimeter for signs of danger. Everything looks quiet —for now. "Yesterday, at the arrest, Wylie called Clay an idiot, said he'd get what he deserved. I asked him point-blank if they planned to take Clay out in jail. He said it wasn't his call, but they could use a fall guy right about now."

I start walking again. Briggs falls into step beside me. "What else did Wylie say during this exchange?"

"He threatened me. Again."

I recount the exchange—the bomb threat, the mind games. Then I show him the doctored photo sent from the unknown number.

"Lane, this just crossed a line." He grips my arm and steers me down the driveway.

Inside the cottage, I yank my arm free. "Let go, Briggs. You're hurting me."

"I'm trying to save your life." He paces, fingers raking through his hair. "You need to get out of here. Now. I have contacts in New York—people who can help."

"Help how?"

He stops and faces me. "New identification. A clean break. You leave Tidewell. You start over somewhere far away."

The words land wrong. Too final. Too neat.

"So that's it?" I hear myself say. "Are you trying to save my life, or get rid of me so you can be with Alex?"

The instant the words leave my mouth, I want them back. "That was uncalled for. Forget I—"

He doesn't let me finish.

His arm hooks around my waist and yanks me against him, hard. His mouth crashes down on mine—no warning, no softness. The kiss is rough, bruising, all teeth and anger and something dangerously close to fear. I taste coffee and frustration and the things neither of us are saying.

He pulls back just enough to speak against my lips. "I love you, Lane," he says hoarsely.

I shove my palm against his chest. "Don't you dare. Not now. Not like this."

His eyes search my face, raw now. "I admit the timing is wrong. I don't care about Alex. I want you. I want you alive. You won't have to hide forever—just until this blows over."

I straighten my jacket, steadying myself. "If you think I'm running, you don't know me at all."

His jaw tightens. "That's what scares the hell out of me."

"If you love me, Briggs, you don't save me by pulling me out of the fight."

He reaches for me again, slower this time. "Then let me help you. Let me do something."

I step back, putting space between us. "I can't involve you in this."

His eyes search my face. "Because you don't trust me?"

I don't answer right away. I don't need to. "I have to do this on my own," I say instead.

"You're asking me to do nothing," he says, his face wounded.

I shake my head. "I'm asking you not to stop me."

Something in his expression shifts—not surrender. Acceptance. "Then promise me you'll stay alive."

I take his hand and squeeze once. "I plan to. That's the whole point."

I turn and walk toward the house without looking back. I don't slow until I reach the back door.

Judd is in the kitchen, already awake, nursing a mug of coffee like he hasn't slept at all. He looks up when I enter. "Well? Where's Briggs? Lally said he was here."

I nod. "He just left. He delivered the news. Clay's dead. Apparent overdose. We both know what that means."

His jaw tightens, but he doesn't look surprised. "And Boone?"

"Still standing. Still protected." I meet his eyes. "For now."

He straightens, alert now. "Does this mean you've made your decision?"

I step closer, lowering my voice. "If your friends are serious—if they're willing to follow orders, not instincts—then I will be honored to lead them." I hold his gaze. "You can call up your army."

Something like resolve settles over his face. Not excitement. Not vengeance. Purpose. "When?"

"Now. Put them on notice. But not loud. Not reckless. This doesn't become a mob. It becomes a network."

He nods once. "Dad would be proud of you."

I glance at the ceiling. Upstairs, our father sleeps, unaware of how close the storm has come. "Dad would be proud of *us*."

Judd pulls out his phone, thumb hovering over the screen. "Once I make these calls, there's no going back."

"I'm aware." I nod at the phone. "Do it."

He exhales, then taps the screen. One call. Then another.

I turn toward the window, watching the pale light creep over the farm, River Birch——my refuge, my inheritance, my line in the sand. I tighten my grip on the edge of the counter, feeling the weight of what's coming—and the certainty beneath it.

I'll let them think this is over.

I'll let them think they've scared me quiet.

They picked the wrong Sutherlin.

And this time, I'm not walking away.

Acknowledgments

I'm forever indebted to the many people who help bring a project to fruition. My cover designer, the hardworking folks at Damonza.com. My beta readers: Alison Fauls, Anne Wolters, Laura Glenn, Lisa Hudson, Lori Walton, Rachel Story, Jaime Campanella, Amanda Covey, and Amy Connolley. Last, but certainly not least, are my select group of advanced readers who are diligent about sharing their advanced reviews prior to releases.

I'm blessed to have many supportive people in my life who offer the encouragement I need to continue my pursuit of writing. Love and thanks to my family—my mother, Joanne; my husband, Ted; and my amazing children, Cameron and Ned.

Most of all, I'm grateful to my wonderful readers for their love of women's fiction. I love hearing from you. Feel free to shoot me an email at ashleyhfarley@gmail.com or stop by my website at ashleyfarley.com for more information about my characters and upcoming releases. Don't forget to sign up for my newsletter. Your subscription will grant you exclusive content, sneak previews, and special giveaways.